Praise for *The Bastard Year*

"Richard Lee Zuras never resorts to melodrama in *The Bastard Year*, but rather trusts in the inherent power of his stark prose, and the complex characters and situations he has created. A haunting debut."

–George Makana Clark author of *The Raw Man*

"*The Bastard Year* is a rich and exciting novel, overflowing with delights for the thoughtful reader. There is terse, eloquent prose, an irresistible voice, and bold plotting driven by scenes that often blind-sided me with their brevity and impact. Jimmy Carter's America is evoked so powerfully that the setting is in effect a supporting actor. Much more than a coming of age novel, *The Bastard Year* strikes me as both a eulogy and a love letter for the nation we once were."

–Neil O. Connelly, author of *The Miracle Stealer*

"The most riveting characters in literary fiction are those young protagonists who must survive not just impending maturity (which often comes too soon) but the complicated world of dysfunctional adults who make the laws and set the rules. Zain, in *The Bastard Year*, is one such character. His coming of age story is told by the author with so quiet a reserve that it echoes loudly in your memory long after you've read."

–Cathie Pelletier, author of *Running the Bulls*

The Bastard Year

The Bastard Year

a novel

By
Richard Lee Zuras

 Brandylane

ISBN: 978-0-9849588-0-1
Library of Congress Control Number: 2012930871

Printed in the United States

Brandylane

BRANDYLANE PUBLISHERS, INC.
brandylanepublishers.com

In loving memory of my father
James Charles Zuras, Sr.

Acknowledgements

This book is sincerely dedicated to my extended family and in particular to my wife Kelly, our sons Everett and Holden, my brother Jimmy, and my mother Marlene.

I would like to acknowledge continuing support from all my colleagues at the University of Maine at Presque Isle, most notably Ray Rice, Mike Sonntag, and Don Zillman.

I thank the remarkable teachers I have encountered in my life, and I gratefully recognize my students, past, present, and future, as they continue to impress and inspire me.

WINTER

1

He walked in like always, tie loosened, briefcase in hand—but there was no hello. I took my seat across from him. He stared at me for a moment, then slid his chair to face my mother. I saw him take her hand and then release it.

"Betty," he said, "I was fired today."

Then he turned his chair back to the table and picked up his sandwich. He took a bite, then got up and went to the china cabinet. He bent down and opened the small doors at the bottom. My mother didn't say a word. When he came back to the table he was drinking from a thick, square glass.

"Eat," he said.

And we did.

The next morning he woke me up early. My mother was still sleeping. I could hear her snoring in their bedroom.

"Dress warm," he said.

I put on my corduroys and a blue flannel shirt. While I dressed, he sat on my bed. He stunk of liquor.

"It's Saturday," I said.

"It's also March," he said.

I didn't know if that meant anything, and he looked in no mood to talk. We went out to the garage and climbed into the car. In no time we were across town and over the bridge. There was almost no traffic, almost no tourists. The monuments were practically empty. We circled around and climbed up the stone-lined hills to where my father worked.

"Look sick," he said.

I obeyed him. Truth was, I felt sick. The car reeked of alcohol. There was an empty bottle of whiskey sliding around at my feet. I wondered if he had spent the night in the car.

At the entrance gate a man in a pale uniform asked my father who I was.

"My son," he said.

Then the man went back inside his little hut and the gate rose up. We drove in, and for the first time I really looked around. I had been to this point a dozen times with my mother those days she needed the car to shop or take me to the doctor's office. But we had always just driven in and parked. Always my father came out of his building, got in, and slid my mother over. That was that. Today was different.

Then I said, "You don't work here anymore."

He turned on me fast. His left hand was on the dashboard and his right hand held the back of my head. I braced.

"Look sick," he said. Then he got out of the car.

I let go a deep breath. Then I puked. I puked all over the dashboard. All over my shoes. On the empty whiskey bottle. When he opened my door he stepped back. He tossed me his handkerchief and told me to clean myself up. The handkerchief was folded, and used, but it was all I had. I wiped at my mouth with it, and my chin. Then I threw it on the floor with the puke.

My father didn't expect any of this. I could tell when I looked at his face he didn't know how to react. Once, when I was five, I completely shit my pants. My mother was at her cousin's house, and my father drove me over there and dropped me off. Just opened the front door and pushed me into the house. Said he wasn't dealing with me. He looked like that again. Like he didn't want to deal with me.

"At least you look sick now," he said.

We went into the largest of the yellow buildings, the one I'd seen him exit from when we picked him up. There was a guard at the door. He took one look at me, then my father, and let us pass. I noticed my father wasn't wearing his identification badge.

My shoes were squeaking a little on the floor tiles, and there were flecks of food drying onto my shoelaces. I could still taste the vomit in my mouth. We passed room after room and I barely had time to look around.

My father was moving fast, and I was determined to keep up with him. Out of the corner of my eye I saw a repeating pattern of colors, and I paused long enough to read a "Bush for President" poster before getting back in step with my father.

When we entered my father's office, I sat down across from his desk. On his desk there were a candy dish and six or seven picture frames. In one I saw my mother in her wedding dress—her long-dead parents beside her. In another I saw myself on a swing set. In another I saw my father shaking hands and posing with a man who I took to be George Bush.

"George Bush is running for president? Your old director?"

"Don't look around here too much, Zain."

"Then why'd you bring me?"

"I wanted you to see where I worked. That's all. Nineteen years I've been here. You ought to see where I worked."

"But I shouldn't be nosy," I said.

"Now you've got it," he said.

He took some boxes out of a closet and emptied them onto his couch. Then he began to stick desk supplies into the boxes.

A large man with a walkie-talkie came in. He walked up to my father and put his hand on his shoulder. He did it in a way that didn't look too comforting.

"Your boy can't be in here," he said.

"He's sick."

"I can see that. All the more reason he should be at home."

"My wife's out of town," my father said. "I've got no one to take care of him today."

"Then you should come back Monday. It would be more appropriate to come back then."

My father pointed to the pictures and I began to hand them over.

"We're almost done," he said, motioning to the room. "Take a look. I haven't touched the files."

"Fine. But you can't leave the premises until I check inside those boxes."

"Zain," my father said, "have a seat. And try not to throw up on this good man while he checks my belongings for treason."

I sat down and tried to look like I might throw up again. The man glared at me and then back at my father. He stuck his walkie-talkie antenna into the box my father was holding and wiggled it around. He told my father he'd be watching us. Then he stood in the doorway and spoke quietly into his walkie-talkie. My father motioned for me to follow him out. The man watched us leave. When we were almost out of sight he told us to be careful driving home.

We tossed the boxes into the backseat and got in the car. My father sat there, keys dangling from the ignition. He was muttering under his breath in a language I didn't know. It sounded Russian, maybe. Or Czech. He kept repeating a single word over and over. I got the feeling it was the word for fuck.

When he turned the ignition the perimeter gate went up. The guard came outside his hut and waited for us. He waved at us to leave. For a moment I thought my father might do something dangerous with our car. He didn't. We drove out as peacefully as we had entered, my father waving good-bye out his open window.

On the way home he talked to me.

"The CIA recruited me right out of high school," he said. "Right out of the twelfth grade. Did you know that?"

"No," I said.

"They held a job fair," he said. "I needed a job in order to ask your mother to marry me. I was smart. Disciplined."

He saw me shaking and rolled up his window.

"That's bullshit," he said.

I didn't know if he meant it was bullshit that he was disciplined, or that it was bullshit that he took a job with the CIA in order to get married. I knew the part about him being smart was true.

"Your grandmother had to sign legal papers in order for me to marry your mother. Your mother was only seventeen and a half. A juvenile, for Christ's sake."

As he spoke, we were driving home a different way from the way we'd come. We passed through the campus of George Washington University.

"I didn't know any of that," I said.

"Okay," he said.

He rolled his window back down. He turned the radio on, then off.

"Is that why you never went to college?"

"I went to college, Zain. I went to Ben Franklin University."

"I didn't know," I said.

"For a year. 1960, I guess. That's all I went."

"Why?"

"I don't know, Zain. I can't remember."

He turned the car onto M Street and stopped talking. There were people on the streets, even at that early hour. Homeless people. People in jogging suits. People walking their dogs. I looked at all the bars and adult shops as we drove. I wanted to ask if we could stop and walk along the C&O canal.

"I want to show you some things," he said. "We never get down here together, so I want to show you some things."

We parked in the lot of a liquor store called Dixie Liquors. I had heard of it before. It was the closest D.C. liquor store to Virginia. In Virginia everything was controlled by the state. Liquor was sold in "Alcoholic Beverage Control" stores. I knew kids at my school in Lorton with fake IDs who came over to D.C. where things were easier.

My father pointed across the street to Key Bridge. He told me how he'd cut through the woods that used to be behind Grandmother's house and come across that bridge to D.C. About how he'd watch the high school crew team practices after school or wander around Georgetown's cobblestone streets looking at the Kennedy houses and the college girls.

He stared at something to the left of the bridge. I could see men sleeping under newspapers on a grassy patch near the off-ramp.

"That's Freedom Park," he said. "Little kids used to walk around that area with their parents and watch the boats on the Potomac."

He reached into his pocket and pulled out a pack of cigarettes. I had never seen him smoke before. It looked strange to watch him do it.

"Economy's been in the toilet," he said.

He took a drag on his cigarette and looked around.

"Most everything's the same in D.C. as it ever was," he said. "If you think about it. The buildings, the monuments, the Potomac—it's all the same. But the people here, the people are changing."

We were watching one of the homeless men root through a wire garbage can in the park. My father crushed out his cigarette with his shoe and put a hand on my shoulder.

"I'll show you something for fun. Okay?"

I thought that this had been fun for us—getting out of the car and walking around. Talking about things that happened in his life when he was young. Things I had never known about his life.

I followed him up the steep cobblestone hill next to the Amoco station. Somebody was playing the piano in one of the upper floors of a walkup. Their windows were open and the music spilled out onto the streets. I remembered how I took piano lessons for one week. I remembered being told by my father that my hands were too small to play.

When we reached the top of the hill, we cut a sharp left and then we stopped. My father started making church bell sounds—his cheeks filling with air. I stared at him and jammed my hands into my pockets. The wind was picking up.

"Know exactly where we are?"

"No," I said. "I don't."

"Come forward," he said.

I took a few steps forward and he came behind me and pushed at my back. He spun me left and the ground before me disappeared. I could see the sparkling water of the Potomac over the outline of tall trees. I felt myself falling. Then he pulled me back. I looked down toward the pavement below—dozens of steep, concrete stairs.

"The Georgetown steps," he said.

My heart was forceful in my chest, and something clicked inside me and I took off. I took the stairs two, sometimes three at a time. I heard my father calling from behind me and the piano echoing to my left. When I reached the bottom, I was breathless and I didn't know exactly why I had run. For a moment I stood there, turning circles, catching my breath. I had seen *The Exorcist* five times since it came out. I knew it was filmed in Georgetown, but I had never seen the steps. I felt, for a moment, transported. I got down on my knees and closed my eyes and I pictured that climactic scene: the final exorcism, the long fall down the stairs, the old priest hunched over the young priest. I stood up and opened my eyes. My father was there on the stairs, watching me.

2

That next week my mother and I looked for jobs. It didn't take me very long to find one. I found out very quickly that by mentioning I was attending Catholic school, people gave me a certain amount of respect. The first job I found that would let me work weekends until summer came was at a local fast food place. I took it.

My mother found a job at a little grocery store that mostly sold milk, beer, and cigarettes. It was a couple miles from our house, and not in the best neighborhood, but she needed something fast. My father had announced that he would not be collecting unemployment. He said he had always refused to take charity, and he wasn't about to start now. He told us he had too much pride, and that pride was important in this life. He asked if I had pride in myself. I told him I did.

But that same week I was trying to be proud was a very long week. My first day at Catholic school, my P.E. class started its section on wrestling. We were sitting in the bleachers waiting to be divided by weight when I started to feel sick.

I got up and left the bleachers. I left the gym. I left that wing of the school and began to wander around. I passed the biology classrooms and the chemistry classes. I passed rooms with maps and charts, and a glass room where the students were wearing headphones.

And then I threw up. I threw up on a wall next to administration. I went in and asked to use their phone. A nun sat me on a couch and gave me some Kleenex and a cup of water. After a while another nun came out of an office and sat down with me.

She said, "Why don't you tell me what's wrong? Are you very sick?" She placed the back of her hand on my forehead.

"I got lost," I said. "It's a big school."

"No one showed you around?"

"They did," I said. But no one had.

"Why don't I give you a map of the school?"

"Okay," I said. She handed me a folding map.

"Mark your rooms," the nun said. "Put a 'one' on first period, a 'two' on second, and so on. Now, young man, get yourself back to class."

"I will," I said. "Thank you."

Then the nun went back in her office and closed the door.

I finished my cup of water, threw it away, and started home. I began to feel better the farther away I got. Past the boulevards, I came to an area of neighborhoods that looked familiar and sat down for a moment to rest. My school shoes were killing me. An old man came up and asked about my uniform and where I went to school. He told me he was "perturbed" to see me being so truant.

"If you won't learn from them, you'll surely learn from me," he said.

He was the tallest person I had ever seen. His arms were so long his fingers stretched below his knees. His neck was long. When he spoke, I saw patches of silver crud between his teeth.

"Zero," he said.

I figured that was what he thought I was getting from my teachers at school. Or maybe it was his name.

"I'm Zain," I said.

"Like the writer? Like Zane Grey?"

"Yes," I said. "I spell it different."

He walked around behind me, sizing me up. He seemed impressed by my name.

"I'm going to tell you about the power of zero."

"Great," I said. I pretended to look under my sleeve at a watch.

"Most powerful integer in the world. Not really an integer. You can't categorize the zero."

"Right," I said.

"Anything," he said, "anything at all times zero, is zero. Anything divided by zero, is zero. Do you see its powers?"

"Sure," I said. "I see."

Mr. Zero started laughing and covering his mouth with his freakishly long fingers. He turned and began to talk to himself as he walked. When he got a few feet away from me, I crossed the street. I headed in the other direction, through a stretch of woods, and was surprised to find myself coming up behind my own backyard.

A man in a black jacket and black cap stood a few hundred feet away. He was looking at the trees and shaking his shoulders around. Then, in a very fast movement, the man squared up and pulled back his coat. There was a movement toward his left hip, his hand went down and back up again. A flash of light was followed by a buckle of noise. There was a cracking sound in the trees and smoke rose into the air.

He turned toward me and lowered his gun. It was my father. I watched him pick up a can of beer. He took a long swig and then motioned for me to come.

I walked to him slowly. As I passed by, I looked at the paper target on the tree. The bull's-eye circles went smaller and smaller around sections of a man's body. There were circles around his heart, his forehead. There was a hand-drawn circle around his genitals. I looked up our driveway. No lights were on in our house. The car was gone.

My father placed his gun in my hand and came around behind me. His breath was quick on my neck. The gun was still warm. It smelled like eggs.

"A man needs to defend himself," he said.

"I can defend myself," I said, though I figured he knew I had never been in a fight.

"Good," he said. "Prove it to me."

He positioned my fingers around the handle of the gun.

"This is practically a hair-trigger," he said. "You don't pull it, you don't even squeeze it. You just fire."

"Okay," I said. "Where do I aim?"

"Wherever you're going to shoot," he said. Then he laughed at this. He pulled his hands away from me but kept talking.

"You've got small hands and short fingers, so they're perfect for this gun. Don't be nervous. This is my Beretta. Twenty-five caliber. You won't kill someone with this unless you're trying to. It's up to you to decide. Those big magnums don't give anyone a choice. A man gets to decide with this: Do I interrupt his brain cells or simply plunk him in the leg?"

I hesitated on the trigger. I aimed the gun for the bare tree above the target's head. I didn't want to shoot anyone, not even the man on the cut-out. The shot rang out, louder than I'd expected. The bullet pierced the man between the eyes.

"Nice one, son. Nice one," he said.

He drank from his beer, then crumpled it and heaved it at the tree. He hollered out, "He's dead!" and clapped me on the back. A neighbor came out on her back porch and stared at us. My father moved back from the target.

"How far away from the target do you think I could hit it?"

"I don't know," I said. "Why don't we go in?"

"Why do that?"

"I'm cold," I said. "Look at me. I forgot my jacket at school."

My father did look at me. At my uniform.

"I remember wearing that uniform," he said. "We didn't wear plain old oxfords then. We wore ties."

"I don't own a tie," I said.

"You can have mine," he said. "All of them."

He stopped talking and tilted his head. He stowed the gun in its holster and began to pick up the debris from the ground. He motioned for me to rip down the target.

"The cops will be coming," he said.

We were inside pretending to do my homework when the doorbell rang. My father went to the dresser and picked up his I.D. badge. He clipped it to his shirt and answered the door. The officer said hello, and I could see his eyes pan down to my father's chest.

"Been a report of gunfire in your yard, sir."

"I can't say there was, officer."

"You can't say? You don't know if there has been, sir?"

"I said, I can't say, but let me get you the number of the CIA director. Though, I warn you, he hates being bothered with this kind of mickey-mouse shit."

The officer looked past my father at me.

"You okay, son?"

"Absolutely," I said.

"You look a little shaken, son."

"He's been sick," my father said.

"I have," I said. "I'm catching up on my Latin right now. I want to get into law school and run a law firm like my uncle."

"My brother," my father said. "Hell of a big-shot lawyer."

The policeman took a step back.

He said, "I'll need to have a look around the backyard before I leave. If that's okay with you."

"Knock yourself out," my father said. Then he closed the door.

We watched from the dining room table as the officer walked around the yard. He stopped near the tree and stuck his fingers in the holes we'd made. Then he pulled the microphone off his shoulder and spoke into it.

"He's leaving. Don't worry yourself about it," my father said. "You did good."

"Okay," I said.

I waited for him to tell me to keep quiet about shooting his gun. He didn't. The officer went by the window and nodded to me. I heard his car's ignition out front, and then he was gone.

3

My father's former boss came over for dinner that Saturday. My mother made pot roast with cornbread muffins and a Crockpot of chili. She told me she had only waved hello to the man a couple of times, but she could see that he was an eater. She was right. My father's boss was no taller than I was, but he was a truly large man. He looked like a retired football player—half muscle, half fat. He was nice enough, complimenting my mother on her cooking and how she had decorated our house. But after he ate—and he ate a lot—he told my father it would be best if my mother and I left the room.

My mother went into the kitchen to clean up the dinner dishes. She turned on the radio. I went upstairs to the attic where my father kept his trunks of old comic books. For a while I read Pogo comics and watched the streetlights come on outside. After a few minutes I heard my father get loud. I heard him say "No" and then his boss say, "Okay, Tom. Okay." There was a metal vent cut into the wall under the window. I put my ear to it. I could make out some of the words, but not all of them. I caught something about President Carter and the hostages. I heard my father's boss talking about hostages in Colombia. I heard them discuss the possibility of my father going back to the CIA.

When my mother came up, I pretended to be reading. She sat next to me near the staircase.

"We're going to fix up this attic. Did your father tell you that?"

"No," I said. "He didn't."

"Uncle Nate's going to help us. We're going to hang drywall and turn this into your room."

She looked over at the trunks of comics.

"Except this part. This will be storage here," she said.

She picked up a Sad Sack comic and flipped through it as she talked.

"Your father and I will be moving into your old room. Then we'll turn our old bedroom into a TV room. There's so much more to watch now, with cable. We thought it would be best to have a second place to watch TV."

"Great," I said. "But it's drafty up here."

"It is, isn't it? We'll fix that. Maybe these windows just need some work."

She placed her palm around the edges of the glass. There were loud noises downstairs, the scraping of chairs. Then we heard the front door close. My mother's head dropped, and I could hear the breath leave her body. I couldn't tell if she knew what was going on—whether she'd been listening, too. I couldn't tell if she looked relieved my father might get his job back, or scared.

She said, "We'll seal these windows shut.

Then she turned her back to me and made her way downstairs.

Sunday morning we all got up early. My father wanted to take us down to National Cemetery to pay our respects to his parents. The anniversary of their deaths was the coming week, and he always preferred to go on a Sunday. Sunday mornings, he said, everyone was at church and not at the cemetery. But there were always people at National Cemetery. Some people came just to see its beauty. Not me. I never thought it was beautiful in any way.

We took the subway from Rosslyn. My father loved to ride the subway. We switched trains from orange to blue and got to the cemetery around lunchtime. The sun was high and the wind was calm, but the air was cold at the top of the hill at Lee Mansion. We always went there first. My father liked to stand on that hill and survey the cemetery. He would tell us how it used to look to him as a kid, when he'd come with his parents to visit the graves of his grandparents. After he'd surveyed, he would pull out a piece of paper and check the grave numbers. Then we'd make our way down to where they lay, leave some flowers, and head home. Rarely, we would stop at the Eternal Flame, and my father would shake his head at the way people still carried on about John Kennedy.

That day my father didn't budge. We stood on that hill for the longest time.

He said, "I want to talk to you about some things today. Both of you."

My mother took my hand. She squeezed it, and when I squeezed back she relaxed her hand and let it collapse within mine. Even through her sweater I could feel her body shake a little bit from the cold.

"People all want to be buried here," he said. "This is the highest honor, in my opinion. Tomb of the Unknown Soldier and everything. I'm honored that my father and his father are buried here. I'm damn honored they served their country."

I didn't know why his grandfather had been buried here. I knew his father had been a Marine. Served in Cuba, I thought, in the '30s. I had one of his sabers in my room.

"I was proud of him," he said. "Even when he died of stupid, fucking electrocution, I was proud of him."

He kicked at some rocks with his feet. Then he picked one up and mindlessly tossed it into the cemetery. A woman near where it hit glanced up the hill at us, then shook her head. People came and went all around us, wanting a look at Lee's Mansion.

"I want to tell you why I got fired," he said.

My mother shook her head at him as he said this. I didn't know if that meant she didn't want to hear it, or if she thought he wasn't supposed to tell us.

"I'd like to know," I said.

"Good, Zain. You deserve to know."

He pulled at the collar of his jean jacket. The wind was starting to pick up. My nose was running and I was hungry, but I wanted to know why my father—a man who never called in sick and worked most every holiday, including Christmas—was fired from a job he'd been at for almost twenty years.

"Things are getting uptight in the Middle East," he said. "You know this, I know. But it's not just the hostages in Iran. It's Iraq. It's Afghanistan. It's Saudi Arabia. It's the U.A.E. It's the whole world, if you want to know the truth."

He began to walk, and we walked with him. We each got on one side of him so he wouldn't have to talk too loud. I felt as if we were breaking the law by doing it.

"They've been after me for years to take a trip," he said.

"You travel all the time, Tom. Already."

"Not like that," he said. "Not a trip, per se. A stay. A tour." He turned to face us. We formed a makeshift huddle.

"They want me, my boss wants me, to live in the Middle East for a while."

"I don't think I want to know how long 'a while' is," my mother said. She said it under her breath.

"Three years," he said. "More or less. Not less than three years, probably."

"You can't do that," my mother said.

I felt that way, too. I wanted to say it, but I couldn't.

My mother was getting mad now. She said, "You can't be expected to leave your family and go halfway around the world for three years. That's bullshit, Tom."

"Look," he said. "For your information I would bring you two along. We would go as a family."

My mother shook her head and stared at the ground. She seemed extremely disappointed with him.

"I already said no, anyway. I'm telling you that's why I got fired."

"They can't fire you for that, Tom. It isn't right."

"Right? Who the hell cares about wrong and right? Who do you think I work for?"

Now it was my father who was getting angry.

"Look where you are, Betty. Do you think right got all these soldiers here?"

He pointed at the massive collection of tombstones in front of us.

Then I managed to speak. I said, "You told us you were proud of your father. I thought you were proud of this place."

"I am," he said. "I'm proud of every single body in this whole damn place." He looked hard at me. "I'm not proud of every reason that got them here."

We walked on for a while. We passed the changing of the guard at the Tomb of the Unknown Soldier. When we were out of everyone's earshot, he spoke to us again.

"I got fired because I had no other choice. They've been after me since Zain was a baby to take a tour. I've been putting it off all these years. I'm committed to go, and I refused them once again."

"What did your boss say, Tom, when you refused?"

"What do you think he said? He was frustrated with me. He told me that. He told me I had shot myself in the foot."

I thought of his gun right then. I thought of taking my father's warm, black, twenty-five caliber Beretta and shooting myself right dead in the foot.

"My boss wanted me out. If I wasn't going to fulfill my duties, he wanted me out. I told him I wasn't taking my family to the Middle East. I also told him I refused to quit."

He patted his front coat pocket. He seemed to be searching for something. Cigarettes, maybe.

"He told me to get out. Told me I was fired, said if I tried to fight it they'd accuse me of having leaked information to the Russians. Wrong or right, for fuck's sake. Don't give me that horse shit."

Right then he looked so angry at us. I wondered what we had done for him to be looking at us like that. Then he turned away and walked down the hill. We followed him across the cemetery, stepping over graves one by one. When he got to my grandparents' grave site, we all stopped.

"We forgot to get flowers," my father said.

I looked at the stones. They were the most intriguing things I had ever seen, and I never could take my eyes off them. My grandfather had died three days after my grandmother, back in 1963. I had been told my grandmother was involved in a horrific car crash coming home from her cousin's house in rural Maryland. My grandfather had a fatal heart attack three days later. It was from the loss, my father told me. He told me you can have a heart attack from the stress chemicals in your body. He told me about adrenaline and hormones. The human body was something my father knew a lot about. The CIA was always testing my father. The machines they used were so advanced, they would come out with readings that doctors couldn't make sense of. They once told my father he had abnormalities in his liver, but they couldn't give him a diagnosis. Sometimes, when we came to the cemetery, I wandered around and looked for stress deaths. Over the years I had found several possibilities. All of them were husbands, dead within days of their wives.

We stood at my grandparents' graves in silence. It was as if the reality of their deaths had made my father's problems seem small. He had simply lost his job, and now they'd be worried about money, which was nothing new. Hadn't my father always said the government paid him next to nothing? He showed me once how everything was based on a pay grade scale. Because he had never graduated college he was graded lower than his fellow agents. Just last year, he had finally made it to GS-12 after eighteen years. He told me the college graduates came in already at GS-11. Some came in at GS-12 or 13. He didn't need to lecture me any further about school.

"Let's go home," he said. And like that we left. The National Cemetery was no place to be at lunchtime. There I was, staring at thousands of dead people and all I could think was I wish I had a hamburger. It all made me feel a little sick to my stomach.

My father didn't really seem to be looking for a job. He had severance pay coming in, and my mother had her part-time job at the store. I worked my fast food job most every Saturday and most Sundays. So what my father did instead was drywall the attic. My uncle got tied up at a construction job and couldn't make it, so my dad got a how-to book from the public library. He was making progress every day, and the first weekend I had off he asked me to help him.

First, we had to go to Ben Franklin's five and dime for more nails and some other things. My father also thought it was time I had my own hammer. He left me on the second floor of Ben Franklin's while he went to get things. There was a pinball machine tucked in the corner that I had played as a kid, when my mother brought me along to buy her sewing stuff. It was called "Classic Comedians." Most of the names I didn't recognize, but I knew some of them. I knew Abbott and Costello. I knew Charlie Chaplin. I knew The Three Stooges. And I definitely knew The Marx Brothers. On the Saturdays he hadn't traveled, my father used to spend the day watching old *Blondie* movies, *The Munsters*, and *The Marx Brothers*. The only one of the three I could stand was *The Marx Brothers*. I didn't care that much for Groucho's overacting, but I enjoyed watching Harpo. He never spoke, but he was still the funniest one. And he could play that harp.

My father startled me when he came up from behind. I was standing there waiting to shoot my last pinball, just flipping the flippers like a maniac.

"What the hell are you doing, Zain?"

"You get ten points every time you hit the flipper button," I said. He had startled me so much I almost tilted the machine.

"Why?"

The machine let out a huge pop.

"That's why," I said. "I mean, that's why I'm doing it. It's broken and you can flip them to get high enough in points to pop free games."

"We don't have time for free games," he said.

"I know," I said. "I wanted to hear the pop."

He looked at me and then studied the names and faces on the machine.

"Where's W.C. Fields?"

"What?"

He repeated himself. I shrugged and started my last ball.

"How can you have a game about classic comedians and not include Fields?"

"I don't know," I said.

"And where's Gleason?"

"Who?"

"Gleason. *Honeymooners*," he said.

"Oh," I said. "Right."

He gave the machine a shove. The tilt light came on. He pushed it again and the machine shut off.

"Game over," he said.

We went down to the hammer and nail section and looked around. They had blue hammers, silver ones, and black ones. They had hammers as big as an arm and ones so small they'd fit in a shirt pocket.

"Find one that fits your hand," he said. "The weight really shouldn't be a problem for you."

I started with the smaller hammers and worked my way up. My father was to my left, swinging a massive hammer as if he were hitting a nail. I imitated him with a seven ounce. Then a ten. The ten felt right in my hand. It had a blue rubber grip and was curved near the head like a helmet. My father grabbed it from my hand, grabbed a big box of nails, then headed to the cash register. I stood there for a minute looking at all the hammers. Then I pulled up my pant leg and jammed the hammer my father had been swinging right into my tube sock. I had to drag that leg carefully as I walked. The women working the registers didn't seem to notice me. Neither did my father.

When we loaded the trunk of the car I could see inside my father's other bag. The things he needed to pick up consisted of a family size bag of nacho cheese Doritos and two six-packs of Michelob. He closed the trunk and then reopened it. He removed one bottle of beer and tossed me the keys.

"You drive," he said.

"I don't even have my learner's permit yet," I said.

"So what, Zain. Do you want me to drink while driving?"

"No," I said. "But I don't know how."

"It's an automatic," he said, "just push the gas and steer."

I stood there looking at the ground. I heard the twist of his beer cap. I heard him drinking it. Then he closed the trunk and grabbed the keys out of my hand.

He drove us home in silence.

4

A long white car was parked in front of our house when we got back. My father pulled into the driveway and a man appeared at the side door. It was my father's boss. He waved at us as we drove into the garage. My father reached over and unlocked the glove box.

"See if you can find me some gum." Then he said, "Never mind."

When my father got out, the man was already in the garage. He was dressed in jeans and a John Deere sweatshirt. He took my father's hand and shook it, then he helped unload the trunk. I stashed the hammer I had stolen and followed them upstairs into the attic.

My father said, "I didn't think you'd come."

"Of course I came, Tom. We're friends no matter what."

"Right," my father said. Then he turned to me and made an ugly face.

His boss walked around the attic and showed my father where we needed to reinforce some of the beams, and how best to cut the drywall to fit the sharp corner angles. Then we worked together, the three of us, all the way through until dinner. We were almost ready to bring my mother upstairs to help us consider paint colors.

Over dinner he started in with my father. He came right out and said, "We want you to come back."

"I didn't quit," my father said. "You fired me."

The man set down his fork—he had barely even eaten—and he thought for a moment. He looked at my mother and then at me.

"This isn't how these things usually proceed," he said. "But in the end, you'd have to discuss it with your wife and son anyway, so I fail to see the harm."

My father stopped eating. My mother stopped as well.

He said, "I need you to come back. We've lost some people, good people, to the private sector. And you're a good CIA man, Tom. You were raised into this job."

"Maybe I'll go into the private sector myself," my father said.

"I'm not going to mince words, Tom. You won't make it in the private sector. You need me as much as I need you. Maybe more."

Then he picked up his fork and ate. He ate like he was making up for lost time.

My mother said, "Tom, what is he talking about?"

"Nothing, Betty. Forget it."

The man looked at them both. He said, "It's just that Tom doesn't have a college degree, that's all. The people who have left all had a degree. Many had advanced degrees, in fact."

"Tom can work in the government," my mother said. "He's got nineteen years in. If he gets a government job for eleven more years, he's got his thirty."

"Look, Betty. I'm not here to cause trouble. I'm trying to help the two of you," he said. "The three of you."

He finished his drink, got up, and poured himself another.

"Besides," he said, "Tom knows the rules about that."

"What is he talking about, Tom?"

My father put his elbows on the table. He placed his head in his hands and pulled his fingers through his hair.

"I can't go back into a government job for five years, Betty. So that's five years before I could even take the Civil *Servants* Exam."

"You never told me this," she said.

My mother got up then and left the room. Her anger came into me.

"What the hell kind of rule is that?"

"Government," my father said.

"Why? What's the point? What's the reasoning?"

"There is no reasoning," my father said. "It's the government, Zain."

"Now, Tom. You know the reasons," the man said low.

"Well, I don't," I said. "That's just plain ignorant."

The man looked at me like he hoped I might get up and follow my mother into the kitchen. I didn't. After a minute of silence my mother came back in and sat down.

"Why don't I finish," the man said.

"Please," my mother said. "I'd like to hear what else you have to say."

"I want to have you back, Tom," he said.

My father stared at his boss. Both men looked a little angry.

"I'm not taking my family to the Middle East. Not now. Not next year. Not ever."

"I understand," he said. "And I'm not asking. I want you to replace a vacancy in Germany. Three years. Then you've fulfilled your trip requirement."

"Germany," my father said. Then he made a clearing sound in his throat. "Where in Germany?"

"Ramstein," he said.

"I take it that's a military base," my mother said.

"That's correct," he said. He turned to hear my mother.

"So Zain would finish high school on a military base."

"Correct," he said.

"You want us to pull Zain out of a top parochial school to put him in a run-down, one-room military school?"

"It's not one room. It's fine. It's near K-town."

"Well," my mother said, "we're doing better than fine here."

The man shifted in his seat. He seemed to be getting uncomfortable.

"This isn't a pleasant thing for me to say, ma'am. But without this job, will you be able to afford to send Zain to a top school? If I recall, the full tuition at his new school is pretty high."

"We'll manage," my mother said.

"Will you?"

The man stood up.

"I've been here long enough. I'm not going to mince words. Ma'am, you can only afford to send Zain because the government—"

"Enough," my father said. "Enough."

He stood up and shook his boss's hand.

"We'll have to think about it. I'll call you."

The man leaned down to my mother. He said, "I'm sorry for my directness. I hope the work I've done in your son's new bedroom will offset my dinnertime behavior."

He looked at me and pretended to tip his hat.

"I'll see myself out," he said.

And he was gone.

The next day we went to church. It was a rare occasion. The only times I had ever been to church were during my cousins' weddings. My father's brother had six kids, and every single one had been married in the Catholic Church. These were full-blown weddings. Two, three-hour services. My father didn't say why we were going this time, but I could tell that my mother was pleased. Her mother had been an avid churchgoer all her life, until breast cancer kept her home. I remember after her diagnosis my grandmother telling me that she was angry with Jesus. It was a strange thing to hear, especially from someone who had hung a crucifix in every room in her house.

I couldn't understand exactly what was happening at church. It felt like every aspect of my life was being overcome with Catholicism. The weird thing was that I didn't know a damn thing about it. At school, I was sure to pretend to be devout, and I tried my best to follow the masses.

SPRING

5

I was standing around in the school's south parking lot cutting class with a bunch of kids, when I first broke my silence. We were listening to a block of Pink Floyd on the radio. A few of the kids were still chanting "We don't need no education" when the DJ came on and said something about the U.S. severing ties with Iran. And that's when I said it. I said the CIA wanted my family to go over there. I told these guys, guys I hung out with only to cut class, that my family was probably headed to Iran sometime soon.

Things happened pretty quick after that.

These guys respected me. They wanted to talk to me. Hang out with me after school. They wanted to know what kind of gun my father carried and whether or not I had ever shot it. They wanted to know what places my father had gone. What kind of people he knew. They wanted to know who ate dinner at my house and the truth on why I kept changing schools. One kid, a big guy by the last name of Bratton, wanted to know how many people my father had killed.

I told them that my father shared everything with me. How he secretly told me about his assignments, and everywhere he ever went. I told them he knew who ordered the assassination of Archbishop Óscar Romero in San Salvador, and that he knew about the plan weeks beforehand. I told them the CIA was in on the mass attacks at the Archbishop's funeral. I told them that the CIA, with the aid of my father, helped get the American diplomats out of Tehran during the Canadian Caper Operation.

A kid named Charlie Abbernathy told us his father was in the FBI. He told us his father worked on the Abscam Sting. He told us his father was investigating the assassination of Mafioso Angelo Bruno, up in Atlantic City. Another guy's father was in the Secret Service. Another guy said his father was a Rear Admiral stationed on the Aegean Sea.

We had broken the silence. We all knew too many current events, and our lies came with the territory.

After school I began to hang out with Bratton and the other guys. Nights I retreated to a house of disrepair. My mother had orphaned me to my father, while she tended a 1950s cash register at a break-even market. My father and I learned to eat TV dinners on pop-up TV trays. We watched Baltimore Orioles baseball games and ate Swanson's Salisbury steaks. We watched *Happy Days*, and *Magnum P.I.*, and ate rubbery potatoes out of sectioned aluminum.

Sometime in mid-April, cutting a class in the south parking lot turned into cutting three classes. Cutting three classes turned into skipping school altogether, and before I had thought about it, I was forging my mother's name on absence slips. I wrote in cursive, with my left hand, making sure to loop the letters a little bit. I used her signature off a cancelled check as my guide. I mimicked the way she grounded her Z like a sideways M, and wrote the phrase, "Please excuse Zain due to personal reasons." We all knew to write that phrase. It suggested maybe you had a disease, or a mental disorder. They never asked us any questions. And we all knew to answer the phone in the evenings in order to catch the automated calls from the attendance office. If they hadn't called by supper, and you weren't allowed to answer the phone during meals, you took a bedroom receiver off the hook. You had to remember to replace it after dinner because the computer never stopped trying. That machine would call your house at six the next morning if it had to. But for all its perseverance, it wasn't very bright. It always called alphabetically, so after a couple nights you tended to know your general time slot. Guys with last names of A's called B's to warn them, B's called C's, and so on. You knew to walk down to the mailbox every day after school to intercept truancy notices.

Cutting class eventually became almost as boring as going to class. Even with the lies about our fathers' exploits, we ran out of things to say to each other.

So we took up drinking. It was a cinch for all of us to get beer. Some kids had fake IDs and access to D.C. But most of us relied on our fathers. For me it was too easy. I'd sneak one beer per twelve pack out of the fridge in the morning while getting ready for school and zip it into the middle pouch of my book bag where I kept my hat and gloves. Before the school day we'd pool our resources and hide the beers inside a hollowed-out oak in the woods near the south parking lot. We always had more than enough to get buzzed several times a week. We drank them warm and ate roasted peanuts from the shell.

My father never noticed the beer on my breath. His sense of smell seemed to be non-existent. The house reeked like a brewery. We kept a lawn and leaf bag in the kitchen. No trash can, just a big, green Hefty bag lying on the kitchen tile with empty beer cans rolling around inside. The living room carpet was pocked with tiny orange Doritos shards. The TV was caked with dust. The shower was growing four different varieties of mold. Everything in our pantry was ready-to-eat from a can or a box. The milk was rancid.

When my mother was at home, she was too exhausted to care. In order to work enough hours she had to take split shifts. Sometimes she'd work until midnight and be back at five in the morning. Sometimes she'd work 8 A.M. to 11 A.M., then 1 P.M. to 4 P.M., then ten to midnight, just to get an eight-hour day. She worked overtime most every weekend to cover the bills.

Sometimes we'd pass in the hall Saturday mornings at six. She would be heading out to her job at the market and I would be eating a bowl of cereal before my shift at the fast food joint. We'd be quiet as mice, neither speaking for fear we might wake him up.

My father slept most days until I don't know when, but he was usually still in his pajamas when I got home. Afternoons he spent blaring his old records in the garage. He built me a desk to do my homework. He built us a set of wooden TV trays. He built a birdhouse. But mostly he drank. When he moved to two twelve-packs a day, I started stealing two, sometimes three beers a day. The extras I didn't hide in the hollowed oak at school. I stashed them for myself in a bramble patch behind our property. And I had learned from Bratton to keep my eye out for neighborhood beer— how to notice if a neighbor kept his beer in the garage fridge. The trick, Bratton said, was to watch for a garage light to go on and off six or eight times a night. Bratton told me everyone locked their garage's bay doors, but no one ever locked the side door. He was right. I took long walks at night, especially on the weekends, and I copied down addresses in a little notebook.

I tried my father's liquor cabinet only once. One long drink of Gordon's vodka put me right back onto beer. Beer, for my father, seemed to wash down everything. Beer went with sandwiches. It went with chips. He even drank it with his Neapolitan ice cream. But mostly he drank it with his cigarettes. He had taken up smoking in a big way. There were crumpled packs of off-brand cigarettes all over the house. When he'd had a few beers and he was out of cigarettes, he went ape-shit. He began sending me down to the 7-Eleven with a note saying it was okay to sell them to me—they were for my father. Truth is, I didn't need to use the note to get them. Everyone would sell them to kids, and I was fifteen anyways. Once, at the Steak and Egg, I was playing pinball and I saw a ten-year-old walk in and buy them from a vending machine. No one asked him for a note.

Besides, I could steal them. I had gotten pretty good at stealing. One of the kids I cut classes with even showed me how to steal Pepsis from a soda machine. It was ingenious. You reached your arm up the chute, all the way up to your elbow, and felt for a can. You found the ring and gently popped it. Sure, your hand got a little soda-sticky, but so what. The cans were horizontal so only maybe an ounce or two oozed out. Without the pressure, the rails couldn't keep the can in place very tight, and you could slide it right out. Free soda. There you go.

It was a natural progression that one day we skipped school and found ourselves inside a Sears. We were walking around the office supply area typing lewd things on the new electric typewriters. People had usually typed something lame like "I like Ike," or "Kilroy was here." Not us. We typed out dirty jokes or pretended to leave messages from hookers. We left phone numbers under the hookers' names. A lot of people from school that we didn't like were probably getting calls from horny guys looking for hookers named "Candy" or "Joy." It was pretty harmless, really, until the typing ended and the stealing began. Bratton put a stapler down his jeans. Then another kid pocketed a box of paper clips. I joined in and stuffed a twelve pack of markers into my tube sock.

"This is why I wear long pants, no matter the temperature," I said.

And they laughed. They all thought I was funny and good for a wise-ass remark. Sears was my idea, though, and I thought I needed to do better than a pack of rainbow markers. I decided on a fancy fountain pen. Then another. By the time I led everyone to the exit I must have had a drawer's worth of pens in my socks.

When we got outside Bratton said, "That's too easy. That's so stupid easy I could walk right out with stuff right here in my arms."

And he did. He walked back through the doors, down the stairs, and returned in two minutes with a brand new electric typewriter. Box and all.

"That's stupid," he said. "Even if someone does see you it's like you're going upstairs to the second floor to join your folks."

He put the typewriter box down next to the building. One of the kids started to pick it up, but stopped. It seemed to make sense to leave it there.

That night my father got comfortably drunk. My mother was pulling her usual late shift and he pulled his as well. His late shift mostly consisted of reclining in his La-Z-Boy and watching whatever was on ESPN—usually Australian rules football—but that night he was listening to old Elvis records and flipping through the *TV Guide*. There was a pile of discarded inserts beside his chair. Any advertisement that stuck out an eighteenth of an inch from the edge was fair game to be torn out. If the ad was printed on paper an increment heavier than the other pages, it had to go. Cologne ads? Out. Norman Rockwell collectibles? Trash. Next to that pile of torn-out ads was a two-foot tall container of Charles potato chips. My father loved the fact that a man in a truck came and refilled his chip container once a week.

Of course there were the requisite empty beer cans. Dead soldiers, he called them. Lined up in uneven rows, some crumpled, others partially crushed. I was upstairs reading *Lord Jim* for English class when it happened. There was a noise, almost a cracking sound, and then a string of curse words. By the time I got to the bottom of the stairs, my father was kicking at the doorknob of the hall closet with his bare foot. I thought about approaching him, but I had learned how to count the empties, and the tally was too high.

I sat down and watched him. He gave the door a final kick and then disappeared for a minute. When he came back, he was carrying the toolbox I had made him in eighth grade shop class. He set it down gently, then removed a pair of screwdrivers and eyed the doorknob. He settled on the smaller of the two and went to work. He placed the screws he removed neatly into a divided plastic box. Then he removed the doorknob and its faceplate. He went to the kitchen and came back with a one-gallon freezer bag. Carefully, he placed the doorknob and faceplate into the bag, then fished out the two screws and dropped them in with the knob. He put everything back into his toolbox, returned it to its proper place, and went back to his TV Guide and La-Z-Boy. It was one of the strangest things I had ever seen him do.

6

The next morning my mother was back at work again. It was a school day so that meant my father would be asleep all day. I had left my book bag in our car so I had to walk two miles to my mother's work to get it. When I asked my mother for the keys, she had to stop checking people out at the register. She had to go to the door with me and point me in the direction of the car. Her boss, she said, made her park on the far end of the shopping plaza. Closer spaces, he said, were for customers.

By the time I got to the car I'd decided to cut school for the day. Otherwise, I'd have to have my mother use her fifteen minute break to drive me, and besides, I'd already missed all of first period. I had a math test to take later in the day and I didn't need the hassle. Every test was the same thing—I got most every answer correct, but still Mrs. O'Riley gave me a D for not showing my work. Every single time I told her that I could do algebraic equations in my head, and every single time she said the same thing. "Leave divine intervention to our Holy Father. I know cheating when I see it." I even offered to do equations in front of her, but she always sent me to the office for a couple whacks across the wrists.

I started the car up while I was thinking about those nuns. Before I knew what I was doing I was circling the parking lot. The steering gave me no trouble; it was sort of like turning a bike. It was my father's 1972 Chevy, with a guzzler of an engine, so it just kind of cruised on its own. I never once touched the gas pedal. By the time I needed to stop it my foot couldn't find the brake and I ended up bumping a parked car. I got out and looked. I could see a tiny speck of silver on the car I hit, but no dents on either car. I grabbed my book bag and went in and gave the keys to my mother. I told her she was wrong on where the car had been parked. I told her it was actually on the other side of the lot.

"Maybe I'm just tired," she said.

"You look it," I said. "You need to take a vacation."

"We aren't going on vacation this year, Zain."

"I know," I said. "I figured that out already."

Then she said, "I'm sorry," and handed me five bucks cab fare.

I hadn't really thought about it until then, but I thought about it all the way home. How every year we had gone to Wildwood, New Jersey. How we always stayed at the Time and Tide. How my parents had honeymooned there, and their parents before them. I think I was conceived there. I think I turned one there. But vacation had been more of a hassle lately. My father's boss wouldn't give him scheduled vacation dates. He'd just call my father on a Sunday and say, "Your vacation starts tomorrow. You have seven days." Once, a couple years back, my father had to call his boss four times a day. It was either that or not go on vacation at all. His boss always knew where he was. At all times.

––––––––––

Mr. Zero stopped me two blocks from my home. I didn't seem to be moving very fast.

"Hello, my pupil," he said.

"Mr. Zero," I said. I said it low but he seemed to hear me. He always looked closely at my face, and I wondered if he was reading my lips.

He said, "Do you know about women?"

I shrugged my shoulders.

"Their anatomy is different," he said.

"I know," I said. "I'm taking human biology this semester." Then I said "Sir."

"Okay," he said.

"Okay," I said.

"I was in the war," he said.

"Clearly," I said.

I looked around for his family. I felt sorry for him, this man. He said some weird stuff, but I felt like somebody should be taking care of him.

He said, "I can do the presidents. In order."

"Impressive," I said.

Then he did them. He did them backwards from Carter to Washington. I couldn't tell if he was showing off, or if he didn't know which direction time went.

"Is this your house? This yellow one?"

"It is," he said. Then he said, "I live in this yellow house."

I took his arm and led him up the stairs. I could feel his bones in my grip. There was a string of muscle leading up his bicep like gristle. When I rang the bell, a woman answered. She looked as old as he did, but her eyes were clearer.

"I hope he wasn't bothering you," she said.

"No, ma'am," I said.

She led him through the doorway, then turned back to me and said, "His mind is fading." Then she closed the door.

I wondered if she knew he could name all the presidents. I wondered if that's how my grandparents would act, if any of them were still alive. I walked through the woods the rest of the way home and straight up to my room. I sat on my bed and looked around. Part of my room still needed paint. Other parts still weren't dry-walled. I slipped under the covers and slept the rest of the day.

My father woke me up. He shook my bed—in the dream I was having I was standing on a plank of drywall in the middle of a baseball diamond— but now my father was pulling on his shirt and saying my name over and over. He stood next to my dresser lobbing clothes at me. My jeans caught me square in the face. I began getting dressed out of habit. I tried to understand—was he getting me ready for school? Nothing seemed right.

"Your mother's at the police station," he said.

He said it like it was a simple fact. I tried to say something, but I just stammered. My father put his belt on and tied his shoes.

"You can finish getting ready on the drive over. There's a cop waiting outside."

I tried to get my foot through the crotch of my jeans and fell over into the dresser.

"Hurry up, Zain. He's waiting to take us to her."

We came down the stairs and grabbed our wallets. The police car was running but its blue lights were off. The officer inside was calm. He told us to just take it easy.

"Let's move," my father said.

"She's fine, sir. I'll have you guys over there in a minute."

I still didn't know what was going on, and my father wasn't saying. I tried to concentrate on the officer and how calm he seemed.

The parking lot of the police station was empty, except for two men standing next to a big blue car. The officer that drove us came around and opened our doors, which didn't seem to open from the inside. When he opened my door, he put his hand on my shoulder and said, "Your mother's fine, son. She's just shaken up."

He led us inside to the desk, then went back outside. My father filled out some paperwork and a woman pinned blue visitor cards to our shirts. The man at the desk told us to wait in Conference Room A. We made our way down the hall, past the chief's office and a fingerprinting room. We sat down on flimsy plastic chairs and waited.

"Your mother's been held up," my father said.

For a moment I thought he meant she was a little late meeting us in the conference room, then I put it together. My mother had been robbed at the market. I looked around for a clock but couldn't find one. It seemed very late.

My mother entered with a female officer. The officer helped my mother take a seat and went back into the hallway. My mother wasn't crying. She had a blank stare and barely seemed to notice us. My father put his hand on her shoulder. It looked awkward there next to her neck.

"I was robbed," she said.

My father removed his hand from her shoulder. He scooted his chair closer to hers.

"What happened? I want to know what happened," he said.

"A man came in," she said. "No one was in the store. A man came in with a gun."

Then she said, "Oh, Jesus."

"Okay," my father said. "It's over now."

The female officer came back in. She told my mother it was time to identify him. She told us we could come and wait outside the line-up room. We went down a narrow hallway and through a big steel door. My mother entered a room with the officer and we waited in what seemed to be a training area. There were posters on the wall demonstrating chokeholds, and one listing the Miranda Rights in Spanish. There was a utility closet against the far wall with piles of handcuffs, shackles, and straightjackets. My mother came back out in less than a minute.

"A formality," the officer said. "We caught him two miles away."

My father nodded. "That's good," he said. "Can we go?"

"You can go. An officer will be in touch with you about court dates."

"Court? This isn't enough, then, she'll have to take time from her schedule to go to court as well? Great."

My father turned on the officer as he said it. Then he said, "And the man? What happens to him now?"

"He'll make bail in the morning, I suppose. His gun wasn't loaded. First offense. I suppose he'll make bail."

My father stared at the officer for a moment. Hard. Then he grabbed my mother by the arm and led her out. The officer who drove us over was waiting outside. He took us to my mother's store to get our car. My mother rode in the front seat next to the officer. She wasn't saying a word. When the officer dropped us off, he handed the keys to my father. He made a point of telling my father to take it easy. I couldn't tell if he meant his temper, or because my father had been drinking. Either way he let us go home. He followed us out of the lot, though, and for a few blocks after that.

When we got home it was 3 A.M. I went upstairs to sleep. I heard them moving around downstairs before I nodded off.

7

My alarm went off at 6 A.M. I couldn't remember setting it and I didn't know what it meant. I started to get dressed for school. I had my uniform all the way on before I realized it was Saturday. By the time I changed into my work clothes my father was upstairs with me.

"I couldn't sleep," he said. "I thought I'd take you to work."

In the car we didn't say a word. My father didn't play the radio and the only noises I heard were the turn signal and the transmission finding its gears.

After he dropped me off, I went inside to get the parking lot brooms and my apron. I had barely punched in before my boss grabbed me and led me to the kitchen.

"You're breakfast cook today," he said.

"I am? I don't know how to do that," I said.

"Tough," he said. "You'll learn as you go."

He led me into the walk-in fridge.

"Get started beating eggs," he said.

He sipped his coffee as he spoke. The steam rose above his bald head.

"How many?"

"Two-hundred," he said. "No shells either."

He left and was sure to close the door behind him. I sat down on a milk crate. I'd had maybe three hours of sleep. I was hungry. I wondered if my mother was sleeping. I wondered if she'd go back to work today. I looked around and spotted the eggs on the highest shelves. I positioned the milk crate for a ladder. I didn't have a container so I used my apron to carry the eggs.

After I beat about thirty eggs the bowl was full. I figured I would transfer them into a big metal chicken pot for storage. On my way to the back line I slipped. The eggs went everywhere. They were on my pants, my apron, my shoes. Before I could get up my boss was on me, too. He stood there with his coffee cursing me out.

I didn't say anything back to him. I took off my apron, hung it on a door handle, and left. I walked outside and across the street to the 7-Eleven. The clerk had on 105.1 and the DJ was having a contest to see how fast someone could bring him donuts. I had exactly two dollars on me so I bought three glazed and I walked the two blocks to the station. I expected people to be lined up with donuts but no one was there. I went in the main entrance, through a set of doors, and then another. I watched the DJ talking and saw him play a record. He pushed the overhead microphone away and turned. He motioned for me to come in.

I gave him the donut bag.

"You won. Pick some records from that box," he said.

He pointed across the room to a huge wooden crate filled with hundreds of albums. The albums had orange stickers on them that said "For Promotional Use Only."

There were albums by Rush, Van Halen, AC/DC, Fleetwood Mac, Led Zeppelin. It was all stuff I'd heard, but nothing seemed to grab me. In the back of the crate were some older albums by people I'd heard my father listen to: Buddy Holly, Eddie Cochran, Ricky Nelson. I started to pick them up, but then I figured he probably had them all already. I told the DJ thanks anyway, but he was on the air again and he just put his hand up as I left. The only person I saw on my way out was the janitor.

It was maybe eight in the morning and I was miles from home with no money. I'd had no breakfast. I literally had egg all over me. I thought about walking home or calling my father, but I didn't think my mother needed to deal with my problems right then. Up the street there was a Grand Union, so I decided to kill some time in there.

I looked over the magazines. All the baseball magazines had been sold. They had some car magazines and teeny-bopper magazines. Nothing looked interesting. I walked up and down the aisles for a while. I hadn't realized I was a little cold until I passed the beer aisle. They had an entire aisle just for beer. It gave me an idea. If I could steal a couple small bags of chips, I could hike over to school and sit down by our hollowed-out tree and drink for a while. There were always a few beers stuck in the back of our stash tree, beers like Pabst Blue Ribbon, and Schlitz Malt Liquor— beers no one wanted to drink. I figured I could kill most of my shift there. Maybe even take a nap.

I didn't have tube socks on so I decided to stuff the chips in the front of my pants. I popped a bag of Lay's to let the air out and crushed the chips a little bit so they wouldn't be so noticeable. I came up through the produce section and behind the manager's perch. Someone hollered in my direction and I saw an older man with thick black glasses come out the side door. The man stopped me and walked me behind the cigarette dispensers.

"You got something, boy," he said. His breath smelled like a pipe. I told him I had something but I put it down already.

"Where? Show me," he said.

He followed behind me as closely as he could. I tried to lose him so I could toss the chips and then lead him back to them.

After we went around the store once, he ran up and grabbed me.

"You didn't ditch anything," he said, "and you ain't doing it now."

"I did," I said. "I just can't remember where. I think they fell behind some paper towel rolls or something."

He spread out my legs with his foot. I put my arms out. First place he patted me was my socks. He went up the sides of my legs. Then he did my hips and my chest.

"I told you," I said. "I threw them in the paper towel aisle."

I asked him if I could please go.

"One more thing," he said. "Rabbit ear your pockets."

I pulled the white pockets out and shook them. Some balls of gray lint fell to the floor.

"Don't come back here," he said. "You're banned from this store."

"Okay," I said.

He gave me a little push in my chest with his finger.

"I should call the cops," he said.

"You have no right to search me," I said.

He pointed at the doors. I tucked my pockets back into my pants and left. I walked fast, and when I got far enough away I tossed the bag of chips in the sewer.

When I got closer to my neighborhood I slowed down. I found a stoop at the edge of a large lawn and sat. It was warming up and the neighborhood smelled faintly of early honeysuckle. I thought about the field trip we took the April before, down to see the Jefferson and Lincoln memorials. The cherry blossoms had been in full bloom. I stretched out on the lawn and relaxed. I was as tired as I had ever been.

When I woke up, I didn't remember where I was. Some kids were playing baseball in the street. My chin felt a little wet. My throat hurt like hell. I sat up and looked at myself. The egg I'd spilled earlier was now covered in light pink. There were little brown nuggets on my shoes. I thought maybe a dog had thrown up, but there were no dogs that I could see. I looked at my body and noticed the trail of vomit down my chest, then I stood up and took my shirt off. I smelled it. I walked down the street and tossed it in the gutter. I couldn't understand how I had thrown up in my sleep. It was something I had never heard of.

I stood there a minute, trying to figure out what to do. Some of the kids had taken off their sweatshirts and thrown them to the curb. I grabbed the biggest one and walked away. I stayed low behind some parked cars. When I got a few houses away, I put it on. It was a tight fit, but it fit enough. It was a Redskins football sweatshirt, and I was glad to have the hood to hide my face. On the way home, some cars slowed down as they drove past me. A couple honked, but no one stopped.

I snuck up to my room and put on fresh clothes. I put my dirty shoes and socks and pants in a bag and hid them at the bottom of my trash can.

Downstairs, I found my father sitting alone in the living room.

"Sit down," he said.

He was close to the window, and as he talked he kept peering through the mini-blinds.

He said, "I want to tell you where we're at, here, Zain."

I sat in the chair across from him and tried to see what it was he was looking at outside.

"The man ... the man that robbed the store made bail. He's out."

"Okay," I said.

"We need to keep an eye out for him now, son."

"Why?"

"Why? What are you, a damn imbecile? Your mother's going to put him behind bars. Remember?"

"He robbed her," I said. "Why would he be mad at her?"

"You don't know how the world works, Zain. You think you know, but you don't know shit."

A car slowed down outside and my father stopped talking and watched it. I could see an older woman getting out and walking up to a house across the street. The car drove away.

"He'll be coming for her now, Zain."

"I don't think so," I said.

My father looked at me and shook his head. It was the look he had always given me when I failed. It was the look he gave me when I lost the sixth grade regional spelling bee on the word "apoplectic."

"You see a man come near this house, you come tell me, son."

"What does he look like?"

"I don't know," he said. "I've never seen him."

"Okay," I said. "Will do."

I looked in on my mother. She was sleeping in their bedroom under a jumble of blankets. All the shades were drawn. Even in the dim light I could see my father's gun atop the nightstand. I spent the rest of the weekend trying to catch up on my schoolwork.

At school on Monday Bratton gave me a "Christmas tree." It was a little capsule with colorful little pebbles inside.

"If you take this right before gym class," he said, "you'll be able to dunk the ball."

I took it. I had gym second period and it was a rain-day, so we stayed inside the gym. The teachers wanted us to do gymnastics, but some of us found a tennis ball and started playing basketball with it. I tried to dunk it like Bratton said and I came close enough to touch the rim. It was the first time I think I had ever reached it.

When I hit fifth period math, I fell asleep. I spent sixth period in the office getting whacked across the wrists by the head nun. She told me she was fed up with my behavior. She told me I had no respect for myself, or for God, and threatened to suspend me if I didn't shape up.

It was late April, and I figured if I could just hang on for six more weeks, I'd have all summer to get myself back on track.

I skipped out on the kids and the drinking the next day and went to all my classes. I came home and went straight to my room with my books. I worked on every single homework assignment I had: biology, vocabulary, math, civics, French. I worked for three hours. I ate dinner working on my English essay. At nine o'clock, I went to bed.

The next day Bratton gave me a bag of Christmas trees, and I put them in my pocket and forgot about them. When I got to second period gym my locker was already open. A brown-suited man I had never seen was going through my gym clothes. When he saw me he said, "Up against the lockers." Then he told me to spread my legs and arms. When he pulled out the capsules is when I remembered I had them.

"Mr. Shale said he heard you were high yesterday. Looks like he was correct."

He took me outside the gym by the baseball diamond.

Then he punched me in the gut. He lectured me on the dangers of drugs. I couldn't believe it had happened. I wondered if I had taken some of the capsules earlier, and I was imagining that this man had hit me.

When he was done with the lecture, he gave me back the capsules.

"Dump them out," he said.

I twisted the middle of the first capsule, then the second. The little pebbles spilled out onto my shoes.

"I know who you are," he said. "You're lucky I'm not calling your father."

8

My mother stayed away from work for a while after the robbery. She hadn't quit yet, but she didn't talk much about going back. Instead she and my father sat in front of the television a lot and watched the news. It was on every channel. President Carter had failed in his attempt to rescue the hostages. My father was pretty irritated by the whole thing.

That Sunday night after it happened he made me watch the coverage with him—because my mother had decided to get out of the house and play bingo at the fire station.

He was sitting so close to our TV set, I wondered if his eyes were going.

"See that? I hope you see that," he said. He was tapping on the glass as he spoke.

"See where they called it Operation Eagle Claw? That's where they went wrong. America should never name its rescue operation after a kung fu system."

I started to ask what he meant, but I noticed he was rolling up his sleeves like he was getting ready for a fight.

"Americans, we're a lot of things—great things—but we're not disciplined enough for kung fu. Not like the Shaolin."

He moved as he spoke. He began a series of slow, awkward movements with his arms and hands.

"And Eagle Claw," he said, "is deadly. There are one hundred and eight locking hand techniques. Many are employed to grab the throat or to lock a joint. To master the system you must learn it as a mere child."

I thought he was opening up to me. My father was showing me what he had learned in his CIA training. Or maybe overseas. I watched him closely as he moved around the room. His balance was off from the beer, but he was managing to put his movements together.

"Shaolin monks train three hours before they eat breakfast," he said. "Can you imagine?"

"No," I said, "I can't."

Then he said, "You used to watch some of it with me, Zain. Do you remember?"

"What are you talking about?"

"*Kung Fu*," he said. "The show. You were ten or eleven I think. I could have sworn you watched a few episodes with me."

"You learned that from a TV show?"

"Most of it," he said.

He stopped his movements and picked up his beer. It rattled a bit when he shook it.

"Come here," he said. "I want to show you a move."

I came toward him without thinking. Then I stopped.

"I don't think so," I said.

He put his hands on his chair and pushed it completely out of the living room. There was a noise behind us, outside in the yard. I heard our front door open and my mother come in as my father came at me. My arms and legs were in motion but I wasn't moving them. By the time I heard my mother calling my father off of me I was on the floor. My elbows seemed immobile. I couldn't move at the knee.

When I woke up, my mother was standing over my bed. I looked around for my father but couldn't find him.

"Your father was drunk," she said.

I sat up and looked around for him again. It was strange to hear her say the word "drunk."

"He didn't mean it," she said. "He just gets ... well ... you know how your father is."

Then she fluffed up my pillow and told me to warm some leftovers from the fridge when I felt hungry.

"Where are you going?"

"To check in at work," she said. Then she dropped her head and said, "I can't just sit around here anymore."

I started to ask if she was worried about the man coming for her, but I didn't.

She said, "I used to imagine you and your father stopping by to visit me. The two of you eating ice cream cones together."

She patted me on the knee and got up.

"You're alright," she said. "You just fainted. That's all."

I couldn't believe I had fainted. When she left I checked my head in the mirror for bumps and checked my throat for bruises. I stripped myself naked and looked at my entire body. There were no marks on me.

———————————

The next day after school I decided to ride my bike. It was a pain in the ass riding along the boulevards and highways, and I felt myself getting a headache from all the rush hour traffic and diesel fumes. People were screaming out their windows at me to get off the road. One guy threw his Slurpee at me and yelled, "This ain't a bike path."

By the time I got off into the neighborhoods, I was bone tired, and it was late enough that the sun had taken a crazy angle on me. I was coming down one of the steep hills, trying to coast fast enough to ride in the street. A car pulled way out in front of a stop sign and I hesitated. I couldn't figure out whether to go left in front of him or stay to my right in case he kept going. What I didn't do was try to slow down. About twenty feet away from the car I stopped seeing him.

Something happened to me that felt like swimming, or floating, then stopped. I was on my bike still, but the handle bars were facing the wrong way. The ambulance man asked me if I needed to go to the bathroom. I told him I didn't think I needed to go.

"Are you sure you don't need to go?" He asked me the same question over and over again.

I kept wondering why he cared.

Then I was at the door of our house and the policeman knocked and my mother opened the door. They drank tea while I rested on my bed. They talked over and over about how my bike was in the policeman's trunk, and that we should watch that bump on my head.

It was a big bump. My mother kept coming in and pushing a blue ice bag on it like she was trying to push the bump back into my forehead.

Every day my mother came in and read to me from *Oliver Twist*. Oliver couldn't seem to get out of bed either. Every time she came in to read to me, Oliver was eating slowly and was just lying there feeling sickly.

My father came in only once to tell me my bike was ruined. He told me maybe he'd get me another one. Maybe the same exact one, he said, so I'd never have to think about the accident. He asked me if I had recognized the cop who brought me home. It was the same one who had come over and looked around our yard, he told me.

My mother brought their tiny bedroom TV, a black and white, into my room. The rabbit ears were good enough to get two of the networks, and I could see some of the UHF channels pretty well. I watched a lot of *The Price Is Right*, and *The Mike Douglas Show*. The news shows were covering the Iranian Embassy siege in London. Some were still talking about Eagle Claw and what might happen now that Carter had tried something. There were people talking about a holy war in the Middle East.

My mother started reading to me from *The Grapes of Wrath* when I woke up in the mornings. After I ate lunch she'd read my history book to me. Sometimes she would stop after a passage and she'd say how awful people had been to one another. She tried to help me keep up with my math, but she couldn't remember trigonometry very well. I told her I had trouble remembering it twenty minutes after I learned it.

But most of the time she came in to check on me she read me books off my English list. We were given a list in April of books we had to have read by September.

One evening before bed she came in pretty late.

"I really want you to get ahead this summer," she said. "It's important to me that you do well. And you've always been a good reader."

"I guess," I said. "I mean, I never thought about it."

"You knew how to read at three," she said. "I used to put you on my lap with a stack of books when you were so tiny," she said.

She was looking past me out my window.

"I would read to you for hours at a time. When one book ended, I said to you, 'That's a good book. Another one.' Then I'd pull another one off the stack and away we would go."

She pulled some books off a chair and placed them on my bed. She sat down.

"That's how you learned to read," she said. "Just three years old."

"That's pretty good," I said. I meant her, but it sounded like I meant me.

"We were a good team," she said. "You and me."

Then she got up, kissed me on the cheek, and left my room.

Things had changed for the better while I rested. My father had gone out and found a job driving a cab. He worked the maximum hours a cabbie was allowed to work per day. He said they were like airline pilots—only allowed a certain amount of time behind the wheel. And my mother started cleaning the house and cooking again, and she hardly ever watched TV. The house became almost too clean. Sometimes she would get up during dinner and wipe at the counters with a sponge. She vacuumed and beat the rugs every other day. There was no dust on the TVs. It was hard to find a crevice she hadn't scrubbed.

My father started working nights as well. He stayed off the radio and away from the taxi stands. He told us that's how his father had done it. All he had to do, he said, was cruise the streets of Washington. He left his cab light in the off duty position, but people would wave him down anyway. He'd tell them he was off, but he could give them a ride without a fare. They'd always guess at what they would have owed and pay him anyway. Even if they paid half, he said, he was making great take-home pay. He bought me a new bike, same as the one I had only blue. He bought us a second color TV for the TV room. He was making good money, and we hardly ever saw him.

9

My father's boss kept calling during dinnertime. Two, three times a week my mother would answer the phone and say he wasn't home, that he was out driving his cab. We half expected his boss to come over and eat with us.

The one night I answered the phone, my mother was in the bathroom.

"Is he there? He has to be home some night," he said.

"He isn't," I said. "We always tell him that you called."

"Well," he said, "I take it by now he's told you the reason he refuses to take you to Germany."

"Of course," I said. "Absolutely."

"Well, tell him I just called to talk to him. Tell your father ... Zain, tell him that I am still his friend."

"I will," I said.

Then I hung up. My mother came out of the bathroom looking for toilet paper.

"That was the newspaper," I said. "Looking to sign us up."

"We already get it," she said.

"It was a local paper," I said.

She grabbed a box of Kleenex and went back toward the bathroom.

I said, "Did he ever tell you why he didn't take the job? Why we didn't go to Germany?"

She stopped for a moment, then went in and flushed the toilet.

"I told you the same night I told your father," she said. "I'm not taking you out of a good school to put you in a one-room, military school."

I went over and stood by the bathroom door. "He said it wasn't one-room, and I think there was another reason."

She came out into the hall and stood directly in front of me.

"Why do you think that?"

"I just do," I said.

My mother got that look then. Like I was intruding on my father's private life.

"We had our reasons," she said. "Let's leave it at that."

And I did.

I went outside that night and looked at the stars. There was some comet or meteor shower or something we were supposed to look at for our math homework. I didn't see how one had much to do with the other, but at least I didn't have to learn any new formulas.

My father's cab drove by while I was looking for the comet. That's when I saw her. She peeked out the passenger window of his cab and looked straight at our house. I couldn't see who she was, but I could see her red hair. Then her head disappeared and I saw my father's hands turn the steering wheel hard to his left, and the cab's tires made squeaking sounds on the asphalt. I could tell he drove through the stop sign at the end of our neighborhood, and I watched his cab until his lights faded away.

When he pulled into the driveway he was back in our car, alone. The sun was beginning to come up. I could still envision the two of them sitting in his cab. I wondered if any of her red hair would be stuck to his shirt.

He didn't say anything as he sat down beside me and pulled out an empty pack of cigarettes. I waited for him to pretend he didn't know why I was sitting outside. To ask me if I was up early or had not yet gone to bed. Instead he rooted around next to the stoop with his fingers, looking for one of his discarded cigarette butts to smoke.

I thought about asking him why he had done it. And what I did instead was pull back my fist, all the way back behind my ribs, and I let it go and my fist came up across my father's cheek with a sound like bone on bone and his cheek split and I saw his skin open up. I saw his blood leak out and his eyes shutting in pain. A dog was barking in the distance and lights were coming on in the houses around us. I felt my stomach moving and I leaned my head past my father into the hedgerow. I sang there, bent at the waist and heaving my guts. My father's hand was on my back. I could hear him saying low that it was okay. I didn't know if he meant it was okay that I'd hit him, or that I was throwing up all over our hedges.

We sat back down on the stoop and my father kept his hand firmly on my back, rubbing big circles and patting me along my spine.

"It's not what you think," he said. "It's not anything you're thinking."

I sat there, spitting on the steps between my feet. There was a trickling of blood from my father's cheek. Some of it was landing on my right shoe. I cupped the palm of my left hand over my sore right fist. My whole body was throbbing.

"Get some sleep," my father said.

Then he got up and went inside. I heard the screen door close behind me, his footsteps making their way into the back of the house.

I sat outside and waited for the morning paper. It never came.

That week at school I found out Bratton had it in for me. Some kid had told him that I'd said I could take him in a fight. But really I knew he was mad that I'd all of a sudden stopped hanging out with him after I'd been busted.

I hadn't gone by the hollowed-out oak tree for a couple of weeks. I had stopped cutting classes. For the first time all semester, I was pulling in mostly A's and B's. A couple of the football players asked if I wanted to come out for the team next year. Those were some of the reasons Bratton was pissed off at me.

But the fight comment seemed to be what ate at him. I had never even made the comment, but every kid I knew thought I had. It was like a call to arms. The day had to come for us.

And it did. He found me at lunch one day, outside, near the soccer field. We were in the second half of our lunch period and it was nice out. I was heading up to the field to see if anyone had a soccer ball, and Bratton was walking back toward the cafeteria.

Bratton knocked right into me like I wasn't even there.

"Hey, Bratton," I said.

He bumped me again with his chest. Hard. People were already gathering around.

"You think you can take me?"

"Look, Bratton," I said. "Why would I want to fight someone I've been friends with?"

"I don't think we're friends," he said.

"Well, then we were friends," I said. "That counts for something."

He put his fists into my chest and shoved me.

"I'm not going to fight you," I said.

He looked around at all the people who had gathered. A couple kids were saying "come on" and "lunch is almost over."

"I'm going to punch you," he said. "Why don't you tell me where you want it?"

"I don't know," I said. "How about at the top of my left arm."

And then he hit me. He hit me hard in the meat of my shoulder. I was leaning into it and my body didn't move with the blow. Bratton seemed even madder than he had before.

Some of the kids were laughing at us and a bunch of them started walking back inside to get ready to go to fifth period. Bratton turned and walked toward the south parking lot. When the bell rang, I was still standing there, rubbing my shoulder. I went up to the soccer field and sat down against one of the goal posts. My shoulder hurt. My stomach hurt. The sunlight was hurting my eyes.

I thought about my mother getting robbed at her store. I wondered if the man had asked her where she wanted to get shot. I thought about my father and that redhead in his taxicab. I wanted to go inside and talk to someone. I knew I had a guidance counselor, but I didn't know her name. There were only two periods left in the day, so I decided to go to the pick-up lot and wait for my bus.

My mother and father were waiting for me in the dining room when I got home. I could tell they had heard about the fight. Both of them had a mug of coffee, and their chairs were positioned to see me when I came down the hall.

My father said, "Come in here, young man, and sit down."

He looked very serious considering all I had done was get punched by Bratton. I got the feeling he'd been told I started it.

"I didn't do anything," I said.

"Sit down," my mother said. Then she said, "Check his eyes, Tom."

My father got up fast. He was holding a big, red flashlight in his hand. He loomed over me and pushed my head back.

"Open them," he said.

He flipped on the flashlight and pointed it straight into my eyes, using his free hand to open my eyelids. My eyes were watering from the force of the light.

"Hold still," he said.

I couldn't. The pain was like a wasp sting. My eyes were blurring so bad I had to turn my head and shut them.

My father said "See?" and I heard my mother say something I couldn't make out.

My father grabbed at my waist, and I could feel his fingers sliding around in my pants pockets.

"Do you have any more?"

I opened my eyes and looked at my parents. Their faces were blurry through my tears and I couldn't read them.

"I don't know what you're talking about," I said.

"Of course not," he said.

When he was done with my pockets, he sat back down.

"We already searched your room," she said. "We found a lot of interesting things up there."

"Like what?"

"Like a lot of things you've taken in trade."

I stood up and tucked in the pockets of my pants.

"Some of those pens are pretty expensive," he said.

"I can't believe you, Zain," she said. "I'm so ashamed of you."

I looked at each of them. My eyes had cleared and I could see their faces. They had never looked at me like that before.

"Tell us," my father said, "what you've been doing."

"Look," I said. "It was just ... for fun."

My mother let out a laugh and shook her head at me. Her hand was trembling on her coffee mug.

"Every kid steals," I said.

My father leaned into me and said, "What?"

"I don't steal anymore. I did it because of Bratton. It's his fault, really."

"Bratton is the problem, then," my father said.

"He started it," I said.

"Started what?"

"He started the fight."

My mother moved quickly around the table and stood over me.

"Obviously," she said, "you are not the boy we raised you to be."

She brought her hand up to smack me, then took it back.

My father got up and stood next to her.

He said, "We've decided to put you in a drug rehabilitation center in Richmond."

I stood up and looked at both of them.

"I'm not a drug addict."

"Not yet, maybe," she said.

Then she turned to my father. "I don't know, Tom. He's saying he's been fighting and stealing ... I'm not so sure he shouldn't be put in a mental hospital."

That was all I could take. I had known boys back at Lorton who had been sent in for mental evaluations. They all came out on medication. I knew too many boys who came back strung out on lithium. No way was I going to risk it. I looked my mother straight in the eye and looked for the words and I told her that he was cheating on her. My father started yelling and pushing me and I somehow kept talking. I told my mother how he brought her to our house. How he'd driven away when they saw me. How he'd run stop signs just to get out of my sight.

By the end of it, my mother had gone upstairs and my father had left the house.

10

~

It wasn't until the next morning that I found out why they had ambushed me like that. My mother told me that the school had called before I came home. There had been a raid on my locker. Some pills had been confiscated. Maybe hundreds. A man from the school, a man named Brown who we thought was an undercover cop, said that they were amphetamines. My mother didn't believe him, but then my gym teacher got on the phone and told her about my being high once in gym class. Then Mr. Brown got back on the phone and told my mother how he'd already busted me for carrying the same kind of pills.

I wanted to explain to her about that time with Brown. About how the man had punched me in the stomach. But I got the feeling she wouldn't believe me. I didn't want her to start thinking I was making stuff up. She'd believed me about the redhead, and I didn't want her to lose that confidence in me.

I was told by the school to stay home for a while, while they sorted through the whole mess. There was talk of expulsion. There was talk of charges being brought against me.

My mother had my schoolbooks dropped off, and she made me sit in my room every day, alone, and work. I was allowed out for meals and a shower. That was it. I might as well have been locked up in a rehab center.

My father started coming by to get clothes and things. I was never allowed to see him. He had taken a bed in D.C. at a men's-only hotel. It was a pay-by-the-day place, my mother told me. I wondered if that meant he'd be coming back home.

My mother started taking things out of my room and loaning them to my father for his new place. She gave him my stereo, and my window fan. What she did was she'd put the stuff on our front porch and he'd drive over in his cab and get them. I'd watch him disappear under my window and then head back to his open trunk with an armful of clothes or one of the rugs from my room. Once, the older lady across the street got into his cab, so he lit up his "on duty" light and drove that lady wherever it was she needed to go.

When I went downstairs to get meals, the house looked different. So much of our stuff was gone it looked like we just moved in. My mother had started giving him things like our wall clock, and her dead mother's collection of Norman Rockwell plates. She asked me what I thought about renting out the TV room to a lodger for extra money. She told me not to expect to go to a restaurant any time soon.

My father said he'd send us money when he got more settled. I talked to him one night on the phone. He said he'd send money and that he was looking into things at my school. They had finally put me on suspension, but hadn't yet expelled me. He asked me what I had been doing and I asked him the same. We both said we had been doing nothing.

My father finally came by to talk and my mother let him in. We sat in the living room, all of us on the couch. My father had already taken the La-Z-Boy.

He said, "You won't be expelled, Zain. It won't happen. I've seen to that."

My mother let out a deep breath of air. She looked more relieved than I was.

"Here's the thing," he said. "They did find drugs in your locker."

"Those weren't my drugs," I said.

"Maybe not," he said. "Maybe so. I couldn't fight that."

He crossed one leg over the other and placed his hands on his knee.

"What I could fight was the severity of the drugs."

He got up and looked around the room for something.

"Ashtray," he said.

"No one here smokes, Tom. Not anymore."

"Oh, yes. True, true." He sat back down and continued. "Okay. The drugs were not prescription."

My mother just looked at him, and so did I.

"They weren't really amphetamines, not really. What Zain had—what they found in Zain's locker—were a bunch of diet pills in a plastic grocery bag."

"Diet pills?"

"Yes, diet pills. Over the counter. Unregulated. I told them if they tried to expel Zain over diet pills they would have a lawsuit on their hands."

Then he got up and went to the edge of the room.

"That is all I wanted to say," he said. "That is the only reason I came by."

He waved to us as he left. We watched out the window as he got back in his cab and drove off.

That night my mother came up to my room.

"Do you know why I'm so mad at you, Zain?"

"I think so," I said.

She was sitting on my bed and looking at her hands. She wrung them as she talked.

"You don't know all of it."

I put down my history textbook and moved closer to her.

She said, "Your father and I had decided he would go back to work. We decided we would move to Germany as a family for three years. They promised your father a pay grade raise to GS-14 while there. A GS-15 or 16 when we came back to the states."

"Jesus," I said.

I half expected to hear some grief about saying Jesus, but she just sat there. She was very still except for her hands.

"Your father felt proud. He told me it was the first time in his life he had ever felt truly proud."

She stood up and walked over to the staircase.

"Your father didn't pass on the job because of the school. He made some calls. The school came highly recommended."

"Then why? Tell me what's going on," I said.

"We found out—your father found out—there was rampant drug use on the air base. Dealers." Her voice broke. "We passed on a huge promotion to keep you away from drug dealers and now look, Zain. Look what you have done to this family."

Then she turned her back and went down the stairs. When she got to the bottom she turned the lights out on me.

SUMMER

11

It was Saturday, June twenty-eight. I was watching the news while my mother slept in. An Italian DC-9 had crashed into the sea outside Naples. Dozens of people were presumed dead. The news anchors were arguing. It had been a day or two since it crashed, but nobody could figure out why it had happened to such a well-made aircraft. How could something be cruising along like that, and the next moment, smack down right into the sea?

I turned off the TV. I went outside to the backyard. My mother had left the ladder against the garage near her flower boxes. I climbed it, and from up on the roof I could see most of our neighborhood. People were mowing their lawns and setting up sprinklers. It was a week into summer and it was already hot. The garage roof came to a point, so I had to straddle the peak like I was riding a horse.

And something came over me. There was a feeling not like I was falling, but like I was suspended there. This was our garage. Our yard. Our house. But my mother was asleep inside, my father was living in a one-room motel in Washington, and I was up on a roof.

The more I thought about it the more I knew how real it all had become. Then, it was like something had been lifted, some weight had been lifted, and I took in the deepest breath and closed my eyes.

And that's when I fell. My fingers were digging into the shingles. I was watching them, and they seemed to be moving and clawing on their own. Each shingle went by—giant, slow moving, and black. Then my hands grabbed at the gutter and I could hear—way down below me—the banging of my shoes against the garage window. There was a piercing sound and the tinkling of glass shards. My body stopped and my feet caught at the little sill of the window. I don't know if I jumped or just continued to fall, but I managed to turn myself around and the ground rushed at me, at my arms and hands, and there was a feeling like rocks rolling around in my head.

At first, I couldn't move. I was absolutely sure I was paralyzed from the neck down. I moved my head around from side to side. I could see our driveway to my left. To the right was the tree my father and I had shot. Two or three minutes went by.

A feeling like drinking a cold fluid went through my body and my elbows came out, then my knees, and I was on my feet. I looked around to see if anyone was nearby. I noted with relief that no one had spotted me. Then, as the minutes passed, it bothered me that no one had. I wanted someone to tell me if I had really been paralyzed. I wanted someone to explain it to me.

My father drove up while I was sweeping the broken glass. He got out of his cab and came over to me.

"Window broke," I said.

He went over to the frame and picked a shard out of its corner.

"I hit it by accident with the ladder," I said.

He nodded his head.

"I'll put some cardboard up," I said.

"No," he said. "Don't bother."

He tossed the shard onto my swept-up pile.

"I came over to get you for the weekend," he said.

"Is this your weekend?"

"I think so," he said.

I dumped the glass shards into the metal trash can and brushed myself off.

"I'm ready," I said.

And I was. We got in his cab, and he put on the oldies station. We listened to Chuck Berry as we drove out of the neighborhood.

"We're going downtown," he said.

"Great," I said.

We drove down through Roslyn, past the Marriott, and across Key Bridge. I could see Dixie Liquors and the Georgetown stairs up ahead of us on the left. Then my father took a sharp turn onto the Whitehurst Freeway. I looked out my window and caught the sun's reflection riding along the Potomac. It was so blinding I had to look back toward my father. His face was clenched, and his eyes were staring hard at the road ahead of us. I followed his gaze, turning to look out the windshield. The underbelly of a car was coming straight at us. I could see a series of connected pipes and tires jutting off at the sides of the car. It caught the road with its rear end and bounced. Then there was a wall of green metal and I could see glass and then the underbelly again.

My father was out of our cab before I understood what had happened. He crawled into the back of the wrecked car. I could see their back windshield had shattered. A woman crawled out backwards. Her legs and shirt were beaded in circles of blood. She stood there a minute. A couple cars had stopped on either side of us. She looked at me so oddly that I couldn't be sure she even saw me. I wondered why she didn't seem more hurt.

Then my father came out. He was coaxing a woman who didn't seem to be using her arms. I could see her shoes coming out, digging the freeway at the toe-end. Her knees took little steps on the broken glass. The first woman was just standing there looking around. My father pulled the second woman up off her knees and she turned around and I could see she was holding a baby. It was little, and I couldn't tell if it was a boy or girl.

My father stuck his head into the wrecked car for a moment, then pulled it back out. I couldn't stand to look at the baby. To my left, up ahead, past the wreckage, I saw a big truck tire lying there in the road. The woman must have hit it and gone up in the air, or maybe they swerved to avoid it. Two guys on motorcycles pulled up and stopped near the tire. They walked across the freeway to where the two women were talking with my father. One of the women was shifting the baby around. The baby was moving now, its feet and arms wiggling around, and she was stroking its hair.

Then my father walked back over and got in our cab. He put his hands on the steering wheel and looked at me.

"I didn't think they'd be okay," he said.

"Me neither," I said.

He turned the key and the car made a sharp, grinding noise.

"Shit," he said. "Already running."

Then he put it in gear and drove slowly past the women and the baby. The motorcycle men were leading them over toward the breakdown lane.

"They were wearing their seatbelts," he said. "That's the first thing I asked them."

He turned off the radio. I hadn't even noticed it was on.

"I didn't even ask if they were alright," he said. "I was so damn surprised they got out like that I just said, 'You were wearing your seatbelts, weren't you?'"

"That baby," I said. "That was scary."

"Yeah, he was in the back seat. Not even a year old."

"Shit," I said.

We got off the Whitehurst Freeway and into the heart of Washington.

"I didn't know what to do," I said.

"Neither did I," he said.

He lied, I think. Everything he did was instinct.

"Those guys," he said. "Those guys are D.C. firefighters. Off duty. They're in good hands."

He stopped talking and we rode around D.C. in silence for the longest time. We drove up Massachusetts Avenue and passed by Washington Cathedral. My father said it wasn't much to look at without the lights on it. We went up Wisconsin Avenue and headed east on a road with no sign. Before I knew it, we were at the zoo. My father took us behind the main area to park.

"See that? That's Rock Creek," he said.

I looked over and saw a bank leading down to a creek.

"At least I think it is," he said. "Anyway the park here and up that way is Rock Creek. That's where I proposed to your mother."

He got out of the car and started toward the zoo. I followed him. There was a little gate open near a back building and we went in. The zoo was free anyway, but I didn't think we were supposed to go in the back. I wondered if we were behind the secure fences. I wondered if we were in an area where the animals roamed.

"This is the best part of D.C.," he said.

"How come we never came here?"

"I don't know," he said. "I guess because you went on field trips in grade school. I was busy. Things like that."

We walked through an area where they stored feed. There were mountains of it, and barns, and a couple of forklifts parked inside a garage.

"You know," he said, "now that I think about it, that's actually a valid question you have."

He pulled out a cigarette and lit it. He took two or three quick puffs and then stomped it out under his shoe.

"I'm trying to quit," he said. "Nasty habit."

We made it to the edge of the public area and hopped an iron gate.

"I haven't really been anywhere with you," I said. "We never went together to the White House, or the Capitol, or the Washington Monument even."

"We didn't, did we?" he said.

"No," I said. "We did go once, all of us, I remember, to the museums when I was a kid."

"1976," he said. "Remember that?"

"I do," I said. "They had that old castle museum building filled with bicentennial stuff."

My father smiled a bit as we came up the hill toward the main area of zoo exhibits. I remembered how he had given me a bicentennial quarter in a plastic wrapper in 1976. Mint condition, he had said. Never touched by the skin of a human hand. I thought maybe I still had that quarter, somewhere.

"That's the original Smithsonian museum," he said. He pointed to the steeple. "Did you know your Uncle Phil used to help run the Smithsonian Museums?"

"No," I said.

I could barely remember Uncle Phil. We had seen my father's sister and her husband maybe twice outside of their kids' Catholic church weddings. My father had never told me why. I figured it was because his sister was ten years older than him. When he turned eight, she was already off to college.

We could hear the monkeys up on their hill. Once, when I had come on a field trip, a few of the monkeys threw some of their shit at us. One kid got some thrown on his jacket. I remember how he just took his jacket off and left it on the bench.

"I've never even been to the White House," he said. "Have you gone? With school?"

"No," I said.

It was a strange thing to think about. I had lived in the Washington area my entire life. My father, too, and neither of us had ever gone. I wondered if it was one of those locals versus tourist things. Like the kids I had met who lived in Wildwood near the beach, but they never actually went in the water. Or maybe they didn't go in because of all the needles the hospitals were dumping into the Atlantic Ocean.

We watched the monkeys for a little bit and then went inside to see the reptiles. It was even hotter inside the buildings so we decided to go watch the elephants. One of the zoo workers was playing soccer with them. She rolled the ball to them and they kicked it back to her. One of the elephants decided to put his foot on top of the ball. He balanced his leg there for a moment, then the soccer ball grew fat and popped. I thought the elephants would get scared and charge something, but they just turned and lumbered back inside their building.

"Game over," my father said.

My father bought me an ice cream sandwich and we walked back toward the cab. It was hot enough that the ice cream bled all over my hand as I tried to eat it. My father made me use one of the hoses they washed the animals with before I got back into his cab.

"We could go through Rock Creek Park," I said.

"I don't think so," he said.

My father started the car and we drove away from the zoo. We got on 16th Street and headed back toward the Mall. When we got to M Street I thought he might be taking me back to Georgetown. But we crossed over M, and we drove east on I Street past McPherson Square and Franklin Square and on over to the Convention Center. We sat there in his cab in front of the building.

"I thought something might be going on here that we could do together," he said. "Like a car show or something."

I looked up at the marquee and at the people gathered around. It looked like nothing but conventions were going on.

"Sorry," he said.

Then a woman got in the backseat and shut the door behind her.

She said, "House office building. Near the Library of Congress."

My father looked at me and raised his eyebrows. I shrugged.

"Okay," he said, "corner of First and C."

We headed over to the edge of Mount Vernon Square, then south along Ninth Street. After a few blocks we passed a sign that pointed the way to Ford's Theatre. I had been there in sixth grade on a field trip. We saw exactly where Lincoln got shot. Across the street we saw exactly where he died.

My father was making good time and we breezed all the way to the FBI building before we got caught in traffic. We hung a left on Pennsylvania Avenue near the National Archives. I could see the Capitol building in the distance. The woman was reading in the backseat. She had her briefcase open and some papers across her lap. I noticed my father had forgotten to drop the arm on the meter. We swung around the back of the Capitol and into an area I had never seen.

Then the woman said, "First and Independence would be better for me, actually."

"Will do," my father said.

He pulled us up to the curb near the Library of Congress and came around and opened her door. I heard her outside trying to pay him and my father saying it wasn't necessary. He got back in and we watched her walk away.

"That was someone important," he said.

"How could you tell?"

"Drive around this city long enough and you can tell," he said. "They all have that same look, you know? That way of being."

"What way?"

"Detached," he said.

12

It was just a few blocks to the Mall, so we left the cab there and went off on foot. The heat outside was immediate, so we ducked inside the Botanic Garden. The air inside was just as hot and wet, so we decided to go back outside. People were gathered around the Capitol, and kids splashed each other in the reflecting pool.

I asked if we could go into the Air and Space Museum. My father told me anywhere I wanted to go was okay with him. We walked those two or three long blocks in a fog. We were hot, and we hadn't eaten.

Inside we took a seat on a bench near the guard station. We took turns at the water fountain and soaked in the air conditioning. One of the guards was listening to a portable radio. My father went up to him and asked what the DJ had just said about Carter.

"Said Carter signed a draft bill," he said.

"So he signed it."

The guard looked at my father like he was crazy. "He signed it, sir. That's what that radio said."

My father sat back down on the bench with me. He dropped his head down into his hands.

"This isn't happening," he said.

I got up and went to the water fountain again. I couldn't seem to shake my thirst. When I sat back down my father was standing next to the bench, staring out onto the Mall. I stood next to him and we watched cars go by on Jefferson Drive.

"Let's go," he said.

I followed him out the doors and back into the heat. We walked slowly along Jefferson and across Seventh Street. My father led us down an embankment to a concrete wall. From the wall we could see down into the Hirschorn's Sculpture Garden. Two women in jean shorts sat on ladders next to a large, naked statue. They were soaping the statue with big, yellow sponges. Families were coming out of the Hirschorn Museum and wandering around, looking at the works of art. I watched a pair of boys play hide and seek behind a statue with no head.

My father stopped walking.

"Go get us some lunch," he said.

"From where?"

"Find a vendor cart," he said. "Get us whatever they have. Get some sodas."

I turned around and walked toward the Mall. The first cart I saw, all the guy had were salted pretzels. I kept going. My body was soaked in sweat and I could feel my underwear rubbing between my thighs. By the time I found a hotdog vendor I was almost to the National Gallery of Art.

The line was long. Too long. There were a lot of tourists wearing "I love D.C." shirts and carrying little handled bags full of souvenirs. My neck was burning, and when I touched it, my fingers stuck to the skin. The little thermostat on the side of the hotdog cart said 105°. I couldn't be sure if that was from the air or the hotdog water.

I decided to get my money out to be ready to pay. My back pockets were empty and all I had in my front pockets was an old Metro card. I turned and looked back toward the Hirschorn. It was far enough away that I couldn't make out my father. The asphalt of the roads seemed to be floating from the heat. The hotdog line stopped moving. The vendor was arguing with some man about his change, so I walked around the back of the cart. There were five or six hot dogs in buns inside little paper boxes just sitting there next to the relish bin. I grabbed two of them and a can of Pepsi.

I wanted to drink the soda on the way back to my father, but I was too afraid the vendor would come after me if I stopped. It felt like I was in one of those dreams where you're being chased by a madman but no matter how fast you run, you never seem to get anywhere.

My father was exactly where I had left him. He had his elbows up on the wall and he was holding a small bottle. I gave him a hotdog and started eating mine. He took one bite and made a face. The hotdogs almost seemed cold compared to the air.

"I only had enough for one soda," I said.

"You drink it," he said.

He unscrewed the cap on his bottle and had a drink. I took it to be whiskey.

"My father's flask," he said.

He placed the bottle in his palm and offered it. I didn't know if he wanted me to look at it or drink from it.

"In Germany," he said, "fathers drink with their sons. Everyone drinks during meals. Grandparents, parents, kids. Everyone."

I popped the top on my Pepsi and took a drink. My throat was hot and it burned so bad it may as well have been my father's whiskey.

"In Germany," he said, "they eat bratwurst."

"The guy only had hot dogs," I said.

"Without relish," he said.

He took another bite of his hot dog, then pushed it along the wall toward me.

"You finish it," he said.

He took another long drink from his bottle. The two women with the sponges came down their ladders and went back into the main building. We stood there and watched the soap bubbles dry on the statue.

"Remember when we used to go to Hagerstown?"

"I do," I said. "A little bit."

"We'd go up there, you and me and your mother, and I'd get the car up to seventy-five miles per hour. Maybe eighty."

He took another long drink, then put the bottle back in his pocket. He turned to me, stepping on my foot as he did so.

"Closest I'll ever get to the Autobahn," he said.

―――――――――――――

It took us more than an hour to walk from the Hirschorn to the Washington Monument. My father kept stopping us to rest on park benches. The day was passing us by, but the heat hadn't gone anywhere.

We stopped again on the west side of the Washington Monument and measured the line. It wasn't quite two times around the circle of flags, but it was getting there. The line hardly seemed to be moving.

We walked down past the government buildings to the edge of the Tidal Basin and sat on the grass under a cherry blossom. It had been months since they had bloomed, but you could still spot their petals decaying there in the grass. Some families were out on the water, chasing each other around slowly in paddleboats. My father finished off the last of his whiskey as we watched. I could see the Jefferson Memorial clearly from where we were, but I didn't ask if we could walk around to it. My father stretched out on the grass and fell asleep.

He didn't really seem to sleep though. He was muttering to himself and his hands and feet kept moving. When he got up, he looked around for a couple of minutes and then we walked along the south side of the reflecting pool until we were across from the Lincoln Memorial. People were all over the stairs leading to the statue, most of them drinking bottles of water they had brought in their backpacks.

"Lincoln was a great man," my father said.

"I think so," I said.

"Two heroes," he said. "When I was growing up it was honest Abe. When I got older it was Roberto Clemente."

"The baseball player," I said.

He nodded his head. It looked like it made him dizzy to do it. Then he turned and stumbled away from Lincoln. I followed him over to the edge of the water. I stood there and watched my father throw up into the reflecting pool. When he was done I knelt behind him and rubbed circles into his back. He tried to get up, but fell over and landed on me.

When he got all the way to his feet, he said it was time to go.

It wasn't dark by the time we made it back to first and Independence, but the light was beginning to fade. We walked around all four corners of the intersection twice. My father's cab wasn't there.

He said, "I must be remembering the wrong corner."

"No," I said. "This was the place we parked."

"Do you see my fucking cab?"

"No, sir," I said.

We walked up and down First Street, and then up and down

Independence. We checked over on C Street, and on New Jersey Avenue. My father thought maybe they had moved his cab for construction purposes. He said once they had moved his car at the CIA. He came out from work and found his car in front of another building. But I couldn't see any signs of construction where we had parked.

My father decided to ask at the subway station if they knew anything. When we got there, we saw a man in a Metro jacket smoking near the escalators. He said he didn't know anything about any construction in the area. "What I do know," he said, "is that when they tow, most times they tow over to a lot near RFK."

Then he laughed and smoked and said, "And they do tow."

"Thank you," I said. "That helps."

The man waved at us with his finger pointing in the direction of RFK. My father walked us back over to First and Independence. We sat down on the curb and I watched him tie double knots in his shoelaces.

"Are we going to go get it?"

"No," he said.

He finished with his shoes and lit a cigarette.

"I thought you were trying to quit," I said.

"Don't start up with me, Zain."

I looked around for a place to go the bathroom. All the House office buildings looked like they had closed.

"We're not going to get our car?"

"It's not our car," he said. "It's my cab. And I'm not going traipsing through southeast D.C. at dusk on a Saturday night to look for some impound lot near RFK."

I asked him why and he looked at me with that face he made, like I was dumber than all hell.

"I'm too tired," he said. "That's why."

We got up and went back to the Metro. My father bought me a new subway card and sent me back home. I knew not to ask if I could stay with him in D.C. that night. Since the day he had moved out, I had never been allowed to see where he lived.

When I got home my mother was asleep on the couch. At first she said, "You're home." Then, as she woke up a little more, she started getting pissed. She told me she had no earthly idea where I had been. She said she woke up and I was gone and the front door was unlocked and one of the garage windows was smashed. Where had I been all day? She asked if my father had something to do with it. I told her no, it was me. I had broken the window by accident and I spent the day looking for a replacement. I told her I'd have it repaired in a day or two. I was sorry about forgetting to leave a note. Then I went upstairs to bed without dinner.

When I woke up I was starving. Most of my face and neck were sunburned and I was so dehydrated I couldn't manage to go to the bathroom. My mother started in with me over breakfast. She told me it wasn't my father's weekend to visit with me. If he had come by, she wanted to know about it. She wanted to know how I got so sunburned. She wanted me to fix the garage window.

It was Sunday, and all the hardware stores were closed. I went into the garage and found some two-by-fours. I used the leftover drywall nails and the hammer I had stolen from Ben Franklin's. The window didn't look good, but it was covered. I stashed the hammer back behind the paint cans we had used in my bedroom. I spent the rest of the day inside hiding from the heat and rubbing Noxema on my face and neck.

That night I found my mother sitting on the floor in the corner of the dining room. A detective had called her and told her that her upcoming court date had been cancelled. It had been cancelled twice before, from some kind of lawyer's request. This time, the detective said, it was because he didn't think the man who robbed her would show.

He said the police had started to take him in on a drunk driving charge while he was still out on bail, and he just ran away from them. The detective told her not to worry, that the man was handcuffed and wouldn't get far. He said they were looking for him.

I offered to make dinner, but my mother wanted to go to bed. I told her I'd get her some water and that I'd make my own mac 'n' cheese and leave some in the fridge. After I got the mac 'n' cheese going, I brought a glass of water into her room and smelled something very strong. Her bathroom light was on so I went in, but I couldn't see anything there in the toilet. I opened the door a little wider until her bed was in the light.

She was already asleep, and as my eyes adjusted I could see she had peed in her pants.

I walked around the room trying to figure out what to do. If I woke her, she might not be able to get back to sleep. What I did was I got some old towels out of the back of her bathroom closet and I laid them out around her and on top of her waist. I left the light on in the bathroom and the door wide open. I wondered if I should come back and remove the towels in a couple hours so she wouldn't know I'd been there. I left her bedroom door cracked open just in case.

Then I went around the house from the outside and tried all the windows. I found one window that shimmied its way up, even though it had been locked. I got a board out of the garage and went back inside and locked the front, back and basement doors. I wedged the board diagonally in the window where the lock wasn't holding. Then I went back in my mother's bedroom and looked for the Beretta. My father had clearly taken it when he left. His spare bullets and holster were gone as well.

I finished making the mac 'n' cheese and ate most of it. The rest I put in the fridge. The couch in the living room was a pull-out, but it was too loud to try, so I put some sheets on top of the couch cushions. I put my baseball bat against the back of the couch near my right arm, and my grandfather's saber on the floor. I told myself to remember to go get the towels off my mother's bed before I fell asleep.

13

I was alone when I woke up. No lights were on and there was no sign of any breakfast. My mother's car was still in the driveway. I checked all three doors to the house. They were still locked. The button of the chain to the front door was placed in its circular holder like always. Her keys and purse were gone. Her bed was how I left it. Some of the towels were strewn across the floor and the room stunk of urine. Two of the drawers of her dresser were sticking out.

I checked the garage, the backyard and the neighborhood. My mother was nowhere to be found. I wondered if I should call my father. The only way I could maybe reach him would be to call the cab company and see if he was out hacking. I went back inside and washed my mother's sheets. I put on a clean set and straightened up her room. I did the dishes and mowed the lawn. I cleaned out the fridge and vacuumed the house.

When I was halfway through my dinner, my father entered our house. He sat down and took a couple of French fries off my plate.

He said, "Your mother's in the hospital."

I choked my grilled cheese up when he said it.

"Before you even ask," he said, "the answer's no. Your mother needs to rest and gather herself."

I wiped my mouth with my sleeve.

He took some more fries from my plate and dabbed them into the ketchup. I asked him what happened. He kept on eating and drank some of my milk.

Then he said, "Uterine prolapse."

He said it like I should know what it meant. I pushed my dinner plate over in front of him. He kept eating while he talked.

"Her—well. How should I put this? Her uterus—you know what a uterus is?"

"Yes," I said, "I do."

"Okay," he said, "okay. Her uterus has fallen a bit. Into her, you know."

"I think so," I said.

"They have to operate," he said.

He finished eating my dinner and pushed the plate away.

"It's a hysterectomy is what it is."

"She peed herself," I said.

He asked me to repeat myself.

"She did. She went to the bathroom all over her bed."

He looked at me like he didn't appreciate me telling him this.

"I see," he said. "She didn't tell me you knew about that. Well, Zain, it wasn't the first time."

Then he got up and went into the kitchen and opened the fridge.

"Your mother keeps a neat house these days, doesn't she?"

I looked around at the work I had just finished.

"She does," I said.

He took a hard-boiled egg off the door and sat down to peel it.

"She'll be there awhile," he said. "Couple, few days maybe."

I nodded my head at him. The smell of the hard-boiled egg was making me nauseous.

"I'll be staying here to watch you," he said.

I got up and went to the bathroom. I thought I would be sick. I sat a minute on the cold tile floor until it passed. When I came back to the dining room, my father was gone. He had left a note on a napkin that said, "Be back later."

I heard him come in during the middle of the night. He was stomping around and talking loudly to himself, and then I heard the television come on. He was watching the news channels with the sound way too loud. I could hear the different reporters talking about the Soviet invasion of Afghanistan. One guy was praising President Carter, saying that a peacetime draft was an intelligent, effective response. Another reporter said it was a non-response, and called Carter a pacifist. Then my father closed the door to the stairs that led to my room. I turned my air-conditioner fan on high and got back into bed.

My father was sitting on the couch working through a box of fireworks when I woke up. I carried my bowl of cereal into the living room and watched him. He was picking the larger fireworks up, one by one, and twisting the fuses until they were tight. I asked if we were still going to shoot them off.

"Yes," he said. "With or without your mother."

"And the D.C. fireworks?"

"I don't know," he said. "It seems like they get rained out every year anyway."

He got out his stiletto knife and began cutting short all the fuses. He didn't like giving them the option of burning out in the wind.

"They reschedule them," I said. "If it rains, I mean."

"No shit," he said. "Really?"

He folded his knife up and put it back in his pants pocket.

"There's a reason they're on July fourth," he said. "Not the fifth."

He picked up the box of fireworks and placed it on the mantle.

"Don't monkey around with these," he said.

He went into the kitchen and banged around for a minute. Then he asked me if I wanted take-out pizza or take-out chicken. I told him I didn't care and he got his keys and left. It was nine o'clock in the morning.

At lunchtime he came back with a large pizza and a bucket of Kentucky Fried Chicken. We ate in the living room on our TV trays. We watched some racing and used the backs of our hands as napkins. When we were done I scooped everything into a Hefty bag and took it out by the garage. He came out behind me and stood on the porch, smoking.

"She had the operation," he said.

"Without me?"

"Without you? That's a strange thing to say," he said.

I looked at him just standing there, wondering how he could be so calm.

"It's a strange thing that I didn't get to talk to her," I said. "I mean, what if she died and I didn't even get a chance to talk to her?"

"Nobody's dying," he said.

He flicked his cigarette butt into the driveway. I went over and crushed it out. Then I got into the passenger seat of our car. My father stood there on the porch a moment with his head lowered.

"Get in," I said.

And he did.

My father took me straight up to her room. She was in the intensive care unit on the third floor. The rooms weren't like they were on TV. Each patient had a room barely big enough for a bed and the necessary machines. There were plastic school chairs in the hallway for visitors to sit on. Most stood.

My father made me wait outside the door while he went in to check on her. A couple of doctors walked by with their clipboards. A man wheeled a big blue machine down to the end of the hall. My father came out and told me to go in. He pushed an orange chair into the room for me, then went to get a cup of coffee.

My mother was asleep. There were tubes and monitors hooked up to her, and I watched for a while as her heartbeat moved left to right across the screen. Her body looked lumpy in the middle where they had piled the bandages. I sat there and watched the numbers change on the monitor. I listened to her breathe.

A man came in and told me it was okay to talk to her. He told me she might like to hear my voice. I told him I didn't want to wake her up. He laughed a little at what I had said. Then he made some notes on a sheet of paper he was carrying. I asked if he was her doctor and he smiled at me.

Then a nurse came in and they discussed whether or not they'd need to place some kind of new line in her. When the man left, I asked the nurse who he was. She told me he was a medical student who was working my mother's case. She asked me if I had any questions about my mother's coma. I told her I didn't. I watched her empty my mother's urine from a container hooked to the side of the bed. Then she pulled an empty bag off the tall metal pole and replaced it with a new one. I watched her hold my mother's head up as she adjusted the pillows.

After the nurse left, I pulled the chair up to the edge of the bed. There was no door to my mother's room, and I felt strange talking to her out loud. I put my hand on her forearm. It felt like cold, hard rubber. Under my breath I told her it would be okay. I sat with my hand on her arm for a while.

My father came in the room and kneeled down next to her. He talked to her like they were in a running conversation. He spoke low, and I couldn't make out all of the words. It sounded like he was telling her the story of how they had met. He said something about a picnic, and my mother in a white blouse and capri pants standing up against an oak tree.

The nurse came back in and tapped her watch at my father.

"Time to go," she said.

My father gave my mother a kiss on the forehead. He motioned for me to do it as well. I lied and told him I already had. My father followed me out of the room and down the hall. An old man with a beard stepped out of the elevator and nodded at us.

"One of your mother's doctors," my father said.

We went down to the parking garage and made the drive home in silence.

My father spent the next couple of days not telling me the truth about my mother. The only thing I knew about comas was from a movie I had seen. That movie kept flashing inside my head whenever I thought of the word "coma." I saw people in comas dangling from hooks—naked in plastic bags. The word itself bothered me. It was an evil-sounding word, and I couldn't stop thinking about it.

One of the days we were visiting her, I snuck down to the medical library on the second floor. There was a book on one of the tables, an encyclopedia of medicine, and I sat down and looked for coma. I was positive if I could understand that word everything would be okay.

It wasn't much help. The book defined coma through an ethical argument about legal brain death. It talked about people in hospital settings showing little care for patients who were oblivious to their surroundings. It said people could live on machines in deep comas for months, maybe years. I wondered if my mother's brain would die.

I spent the rest of the day in the hospital's chapel. It was no bigger than our living room. There were a couple of chairs and an altar. There were a few copies of the Bible, and a place to light candles. In the center, above the altar, was a stained-glass window of Jesus. Behind Jesus was a brick wall.

I had learned enough Catholicism in school to know how to pray. I knew what to say, how to position my body, how to move. Instead, I just sat there. Any god had to know why I was all of a sudden in a makeshift church. Any god would know the reasons for my sudden conversion. Any god would know I was a fraud. It felt warm, though, to sit there—all alone with a painting of Christ and a candle I lit and watched until it died into a sudden pile of wax.

My father decided it was time to light the fireworks. The sky was still bright with the sun that had been out all day. Even in the shade of our house, the air was uncomfortable. Record temperatures had been reached all week in Virginia, and the coming night skies barely seemed to help.

My father had gotten ahold of some jumping jacks and ladyfingers at a Korean market in South Arlington. He taught me how to light them and wait. We waited until we heard the sputtering of the internal fuses and then we let them go. They shot screaming off into the sky and we watched as they danced and exploded above our heads. We lit dozens of them. Maybe hundreds. And for a while there was nothing else but the noise and shower of sparks that we created.

And then it was over. The morning came and we were back in the car to start all over again. On the way to the hospital, we stopped and waited in a one-hour line for gas. We also stopped for breakfast. We talked about heading down to D.C. for the celebrations, to hear the military band play the "Star Spangled Banner." But we kept driving. At the hospital we parked and went in as usual to see her.

She was gone. We stood outside her room in intensive care and saw nothing but a couple of machines. Not even her bed. My father looked at me and his face went down. My muscles felt loose and I held to the door for support. A nurse walked by and said, matter-of-factly, that she had been moved to a recovery room on the fourth floor. Then she said that someone should have called us.

My father just headed for the stairs and I followed him. We walked past the administration desks and the nurses' stations. No one badgered us about the rules or whether it was visiting hour. My mother was right there in front of us, her bed being wheeled into a private room with windows. The two men rolling her bed locked down her wheels and left. My mother wasn't saying anything, but it was clear she was awake. A nurse came in and set up a few things. No one came in with any breathing machines.

We sat with her and watched her move. My father stroked her hair. There were lots of raw marks on her arms and around her mouth, but the coma was gone.

14

My mother returned to our house the day seven people were crushed to death in Brazil while trying to meet the Pope. We didn't talk about it. We didn't talk about the fact that our grass, and the grass in all the yards of our neighbors, was brown and dead. We didn't talk about the rolling blackouts, the gas station lines, or the hostages. We did dote on my mother. My father bought a tray for her to eat off of in bed. We placed a flower in a tiny vase on the tray when we brought it to her room. The older woman across the street had heard, and she brought us bean casseroles, homemade pies, and ham sandwiches.

My mother mostly slept. When she was awake, she watched whatever was on TV and we ran the vacuum and washed the dishes. When she fell back asleep, we read the newspaper or watched sports in the TV room with the sound turned down. We snuck outside at night to water her dying flower gardens, while it was cool, and so none of our neighbors would catch us wasting water.

And my father quit drinking. He boxed up all his beer and his liquor and he stored it in the little basement area near the furnace. Quitting did some things to him. He ate more. He showered more. And he got hot more. We had placed power saver stickers on the central air—where to set it during the day, and where it should go at night. My father began to ignore the guidelines. It was getting hotter outside and colder inside. Until the power went out.

At first we thought we had blown a fuse or fried a wire. I went outside into the heat. I walked around the neighborhood and peered into the houses. I listened for the racket of the window units. But the power was out as far as I could see. I came home and accused my father of doing it by turning our central air up so high.

"There is a power shortage," I said.

"You're an idiot," he said.

And like that, everything changed again. My mother grew uncomfortable boxed up like that in their room. My upstairs bedroom shot up to one hundred degrees in a matter of hours. My father fished out his whiskey and dumped it over the last of the melting ice cubes. The milk in the fridge went sour.

That night, my father gave my mother some sleeping pills. He spent the evening outside on the porch, smoking his cigarettes and drinking his warm beers. I opened every window in the house and slept with my naked body plastered against the freshly painted wall.

The next day my father pulled batteries out of his old camping gear and powered up the radio. We listened to it in their bedroom. My father kept my mother on her pills, and we took turns fanning her and wiping her arms and legs with a wet sponge. We listened to the oldies station, and when it wasn't his turn to fan her, my father rocked back and forth to the music of the 50s, of his childhood, and he drank his liquor.

It cooled off enough at dusk that I could take a walk. Power trucks were working a few blocks away. I sat on a curb and watched men go in and out of a fenced area that housed giant metal rods. People were out on the stoops of their houses. Some looked like they were praying.

I kept walking. I walked past the houses where I used to steal beer. Past the woods where they stretched out of our neighborhood. I watched a man in his garage, struggling to get a generator started. Another man was standing in his yard spraying his kids with a hose. I saw an older woman trying to push a lawn mower up the porch stairs into her house.

I went up behind her and offered to help.

"Thank you," she said. But she wouldn't take her hands off the mower.

"If you hold the door," I said, "I'll push the mower inside."

"Okay," she said.

She went up the stairs and opened the door to her house. Even in the late-day heat, even from the bottom of her porch stairs, I could smell something horrible coming from inside. I got the mower into the house and into the hallway. The smell was even stronger. The woman said something behind me but I couldn't make it out. I was staring at a man lying face up on a sofa. He seemed to be almost sunken into the cushions. There were black flies on his face and his chest. He wasn't moving.

I leaned into the living room and sniffed at the air. The smell was definitely coming from him. I turned to the woman and started shaking my head no at her. She tilted her head and smiled at me. Her eyes were wet. I put my shirt up over my mouth and nose and went toward the couch. I waved at the flies but they wouldn't budge.

"He's dead," I said. "Is this your husband? He's dead."

"It's okay," she said.

I looked at him again. His face seemed familiar.

"Who is he?"

"My husband," she said. "Fifty years."

"No," I said, "I mean who is he? I think I know him."

I looked at her. She was crying noticeably.

"I'm sorry," I said. "Fifty years. That's something."

I put two fingers under his ear. Nothing. My fingers looked like toothpicks against his neck. I pulled his arm up and looked at his long fingers. It was Mr. Zero.

"I'm sorry," I said.

I went to her and put my hand on her shoulder. I remembered her eyes.

"He's really dead," I said. "We should call somebody."

She looked at me like my father always did. Like I was an idiot.

"I called the authorities," she said. "Every one of them."

I nodded my head. I kneeled down next to her.

"Where are they?"

"They said they would come as soon as possible," she said. "Everything is backed up from the heat wave, and the power is out from Baltimore to Richmond."

"I didn't know," I said. "Do you need anything?"

She smiled at me and patted my hand.

"Thank you for bringing in the lawn mower," she said.

She led me to the door. She told me her husband had talked about me the day he died. Then she waved goodbye at me and closed the door.

When I got home, our power was back on. My father was in the kitchen going through the refrigerator, pulling out all the food and the jars. I sat down at the table and watched him. He kept an open bottle of beer in one hand and used the other hand to move the items.

"I think we should talk," I said.

"Sure," he said. He screwed the top off a container of ketchup and smelled it. He wrinkled his nose and then placed it back on the fridge door. He took the last swallow of his beer and tossed the bottle in the sink. Then he sat down in front of the fridge.

"People died in this heat," I said.

"People are always dying," he said. "You can count on that."

He grabbed a few more jars and opened them.

"Mother didn't die," I said.

"No," he said, "she didn't."

He stood up and grabbed his car keys and another beer.

"Put all the stuff back how it was unless it's rotten," he said.

"Where are you going?"

"Elsewhere," he said.

He gave me a pat on the shoulder as he passed by. I watched him out the window as he started the car and drove away.

I took my mother a glass of water and an apple I found in the back of the fridge. The air conditioning was back on, full strength, and even in her sleep she looked happy to have it. I put the apple down next to the water and shut the door to her room. I went out in the street and looked around. No one was outside anymore. Lights were coming on all around me. The night was filled with the humming of air conditioners.

FALL

15

By the time the heat wave ended in September, a lot of things had happened that my mother and father weren't talking about. The Americans had boycotted the Moscow Olympics. The newspaper had seduced us with a made-up story about a heroin addict. A dingo in Australia had supposedly disappeared with a baby. And my father had become a dangerous drunk.

My mother and my father, in fact, were barely talking about anything. After Reagan won the nomination, my mother learned that the party no longer supported the equal rights amendment for women. My father said it didn't matter. He said that women had come so far they didn't need that kind of protection anymore. My mother told him Reagan was too close to the religious communities. My father didn't see a problem with a little more religion in Washington. My mother asked if that were true, then why hadn't he supported John Kennedy? It all went to hell from there.

And that was family dinner for a while, until it wasn't anymore. We began to eat at different times. We made our own meals in the microwave and taped our names to our Tupperware leftovers. We ate in different rooms and watched different shows. When we did watch *Dallas* re-runs together, we never discussed who might have shot J.R..

In school I studied pre-calculus, archaic vocabulary words, and how to make a perfectly lined, multi-colored, acrylic pyramid. No one in school talked about the Iran-Iraq war, and only in passing did anyone mention the hostages. These things were not big topics in a school where the teachers wore habits while preaching to us about the importance of thirteen-hundred SAT test scores.

As the November elections approached, my mother and father barely slept in the same room. My father began to drive his cab at odd hours, when he felt sober enough. Sometimes he'd drink himself to sleep after dinner and go out hacking from midnight to dawn. My mother and I never talked about his drinking. We never came close to saying the word "alcoholic."

My mother, in short, became a hopeful Democrat, and in our family that was an even more dangerous word. My father had told me years earlier, in passing, that I could grow up and vote however I wanted to. No pressure, he said. I wondered even then how many boys grew up to vote differently from their fathers. I had been sure to vote Republican when we held our mock election in junior high in '76. The Republicans lost, but it had been very close. I remember Carter beating Ford by about a hundred votes. I wondered why, as we were getting older, we had stopped discussing politics in our classrooms. Maybe kids were doing it in the public schools, but I didn't know.

We did eat dinner together the night of the election. My mother made shepherd's pie and my father had bought some pistachio ice cream. We talked about the weather and when we thought the leaves would fall off the trees like we were strangers waiting to catch a bus. After dinner we watched the election coverage, my father switching from CBS to ABC to NBC and eventually to cable. But it was over before it started. My father seemed to be switching channels in order to find a closer race. My mother just stared at the television like she couldn't believe it. Carter barely held a lead in any state.

"Sometimes," my father said, "these things turn around. It's all about precincts."

"No," my mother said. "You won."

My father put down the remote and then walked over to turn off the TV.

"I didn't win," he said. "Reagan did."

My mother got up and looked right at me, and then at my father.

"Bush is in," she said. "Your man's the new vice-president of the United States."

My father nodded at her and cleared his throat.

My mother walked into her bedroom and shut the door. I sat down and watched our bowls of ice cream melt.

"It was exactly one year ago today," my father said, "that the hostages were taken."

He looked at me as if he wanted me to say something. I figured he was probably wrong about it being a year to the day, but I wasn't about to tell him that. He took a spoonful of his melted pistachio ice cream and ate it. Maybe he was right, though, about the year. It seemed like maybe he had put some thought into it.

"A year is a long time," he said. "A lot can happen in a year."

I nodded. I hadn't really thought too much about it. About what they did during all that time.

"I think," he said, "they're a kind of family now. All those different people."

"It really bothers you," I said. "Doesn't it?"

He ate some more ice cream out of his bowl. Then he ate some of mine.

"This tastes like shit," he said.

He stacked the bowls up and took them into the kitchen. Then I heard him go out the back door. I wondered if I should talk to him, or if he wanted to be alone. I turned the TV back on and flipped around the news stations. They were already calling the election a landslide. I shut it off and went to listen at my mother's door. It seemed like she had already gone to sleep. Halfway up my stairs I wondered again if my father had meant for me to follow him outside.

When I got out the back door I saw two men, one chasing the other through the woods. My father yelled for me to help him, his voice loud and sharp. I ran to where I thought the man would break through a bluff of pines and I dove and nicked his leg with my forearm. Then my father was on him, swinging his fists into the man's back and sides. The man's body was writhing after each hit, trying to coil up and guard against the next one. I grabbed my father at the neck and pulled until he came off, and the man kicked his way out of there, falling again and again as he ran away.

My father was breathing like a madman. His knuckles were bleeding on both hands. He was screaming to himself, "I knew we were being watched," and "I knew it. I knew it." I kept my arms around his chest, afraid he would turn and swing at me for what I had done.

Lights came on in the houses next to ours, and then our back porch light. My father kept breathing hard and I wondered if my mother would manage to hear us. She stood there a moment with her hands on the railing, then turned the light off and went back inside. My father pushed me off of him and stood up. His shirt was torn from the fight, and there were flashes of his blood where he had wiped his knuckles on the fabric. He walked slowly back to the house. I didn't follow him.

My father spent the next few days at home. He didn't leave to drive his cab. He didn't leave to buy groceries. During the day he sat near the windows and peeked out through the curtains. When he took a shower, he left the bathroom door open and the window shade rolled up. I was allowed to go to school, and school only. A friend of his at the cab company picked me up and dropped me off. My mother wasn't allowed to leave the house.

I knew better than to ask him who he thought he had beaten up, or who he thought was still watching us. For my part, I was sure he had beaten up some guy who happened to be walking home through the woods. I was hopeful that whoever that man was, he wouldn't press charges against me and my father.

My father barely seemed to eat anything. He'd have a hard-boiled egg for dinner and maybe a frosted Pop-Tart for lunch. I never saw him eat breakfast. He started sleeping in different parts of the house each night. One night he fell asleep on the floor of the garage. My mother took a job stuffing envelopes for local companies at ten for a penny. At night I sat with her at the dining room table. I did my math homework and read *Catch-22* for English class. When she got tired, I helped her seal the envelopes with a tiny wet sponge. It was tedious work, and it was beginning to show on her.

My father started wearing his gun the week after he'd beaten that man. He wore it on his chest over his T-shirt. He told me it was loaded and chambered. He told me not to touch it.

The older woman across the street stopped by two weeks before Thanksgiving. My father let her in and my mother brought her a cup of peppermint tea and an old shortbread cookie. Up close, she didn't seem so old. They sat in the living room and talked pleasantly about anything they could think of.

Then she said, "I'm wondering if something is amiss here."

My father practically spit out his beer. My mother didn't move a muscle.

"We're all fine here," my father said.

"Oh," she said. "I'm happy to hear that. There is concern, in the neighborhood."

My mother got up and poured her some more tea. Then my mother poured an extra cup and brought it to me. I took a sip. It smelled better than it tasted.

"It's just that no one ever seems to come and go," she said. "Except your boy in a cab."

My father looked at her and smiled. She drank her tea.

"Car's broken," he said. "And we've been a little sick."

"I see," she said. "But you're all better now?"

"We are," he said.

Then he lifted his arm and checked his watch.

"I really should be going," she said. "I have a roast in the oven."

My father placed his hand in the small of her back and helped her through the hall. He thanked her for stopping by and closed the front door softly behind her. The three of us looked at one another for a moment, then made our way into separate rooms of the house.

16

On Saturday we needed groceries. My father gave me the list and the car keys. I had my learner's permit, and I was nervous about driving alone. Then he changed his mind, he said, because our bank account was empty. He said he needed to somehow buy the groceries without any cash.

My mother and I sat at the kitchen table and picked at bowls of dry cereal.

"We could use orange juice," she said.

"That's gross," I said.

She poured the rest of the orange juice into her glass and drank it.

"My father," she said, "used to pour orange juice over his corn flakes when he was a kid."

I wondered what orange juice might taste like over corn flakes. It made me feel sick to think about it.

"Cereal wasn't sweetened then like it is today," she said.

"That's still pretty gross," I said.

"Like milk and Pepsi," she said.

"I tried that once."

"I never could," she said.

It was the first time my father had left the house in weeks. I wondered when my mother last left.

I asked, "That man, the robber. Did he have blondish hair? Kind of hairy sideburns?"

She pushed her bowl away and shook her head no.

"A mustache?"

"No," she said.

Then she said, "I don't know. I can't remember."

"I think I might have seen a man that could have been the robber."

My mother stood up and went to the fridge. She opened the door, looked around, then closed it.

"Doesn't sound like him," she said.

"Which part?"

"Any of it," she said.

She came and sat back down across from me.

"Zain, why are you asking?"

"Because I saw a man," I said. "It's possible it was the man that robbed you."

"It wasn't, Zain. Whoever you saw or whatever you're talking about, it wasn't him," she said.

And she left the room.

The next day I got up and walked over to the oak tree at school. I didn't know if Bratton and the other guys were still stashing beers there or not. I hardly ever saw Bratton, and when I did, we just sort of nodded our heads at each other. But they were there, those beers. In the back of the tree were dirty cans of Pabst and some cheap-looking brands I had never heard of. I carried as many home as I could fit in my backpack. I stopped by a 7-Eleven and grabbed a five-pound bag of ice and a two-dollar Styrofoam cooler. I hauled it all into our garage and set up shop.

By the time the football games came on my beers were cold, and I was ready. My father was set up in his La-Z-Boy, beer in hand. He had the volume turned down so he could listen for suspicious sounds outside our house. Every time a commercial came on, he went through the house and peeked out all our windows. My mother was taking a long bath. I could hear her listening to Merle Haggard. The wall between the living room and bathroom vibrated with thick, country bass.

I grabbed a bag of taco-flavored Doritos and sat down on the couch. I popped open a Pabst Blue Ribbon and took a drink. My father didn't seem to notice. I took a few more drinks and ate some Doritos. Nothing. I took a long drink and then let out a nasty belch. My father didn't say a word.

I wondered if he saw me, or if he thought I had a can of Pepsi. I finished the beer and popped another. My father did the same. When he walked by me to go to the fridge he didn't say anything. When he got up to look out the windows he still didn't say anything. Finally, I walked over to the TV, put my can of beer on top of it, and changed the station from the NFC game to the AFC game. I called the score out to him, then changed the channel back to the game we were watching. When I went back to the couch, I purposefully left my beer on the TV. I sat down and ate a few more Doritos.

Five minutes went by. Then ten minutes. The commercials came on and my father went out to make his rounds. He came back with a big can of potato sticks, and another can of beer. I started to mirror him. When he got a new beer, so did I. When he drank, I drank. We drank all through the game, even through the halftime show. The West Coast game came on. We kept drinking.

My mother came in to see if I had made myself some dinner. She stood there, in the middle of us, looking at all of our empty cans. Dead soldiers. I saw her lips moving. It looked like she was counting them up.

"That's it," she said.

She looked at my father when she said it. Then she walked into the dining room. I heard the sound of her keys. Then she said "stupid bastard" very loud. My father didn't get up.

"She'll be back," he said.

"You don't know that," I said.

"I do," he said. "I have her only car key on my key ring."

I stood up to look out the window. I came down pretty fast—my balance was nowhere and my legs weren't helping. My mother came back in and shut off the TV. She shook her head at me. Then she turned to face him. She took a step and pointed her finger.

"This stops here," she said.

My father put down his beer and crossed his legs. They stared at each other for some time. I waited for her to say something else. I wondered if she couldn't say it to him.

I said, "I'm an alcoholic."

They turned on me, and my father knocked over his little table in the process. His beer went sideways on the floor, sloshing out.

"I am," I said. "And I need someone to take me to an AA meeting."

"I'm not taking you," he said.

"I can't believe this," she said.

My father got up and stood next to my mother.

"One of you will have to," I said. "I'm not old enough to go by myself."

"I'll take you," she said.

"The hell you will," he said. "I will."

And like that, my father forgot about leaving my mother alone in the house. He started calling places, one after the next, looking for a meeting. Then he told me to go take a shower.

"We're going to a meeting tonight," he said.

We drove to a midnight meeting at a community center in Alexandria. The room it was in was underground, and we had to go down a spiral staircase to get there. A sign by the door said, "Do not enter unless you are sober." I asked my father if he thought everyone obeyed that. He shook his head no. There were metal folding chairs circled around the edges of the room. A couple of men were sitting and reading Bibles. One man in the corner kept pulling his hands through his hair like he was ripping it out. My father led me to a buffet table at the back of the room. There were boxes of Krispy Kreme glazed doughnuts and three pots of coffee. All the pots had masking tape across them with the word "strong" written on them.

A man in a black suit shook my father's hand, and then mine.

"Welcome," he said.

I said thank you under my breath. My father picked up a glazed doughnut and handed it to me.

"I'm not hungry," I said.

He tossed the doughnut into the lid of the box.

The men started taking their seats and we did too. The man in the black suit sat at a desk up front. He looked around the room and nodded at most of the men. He didn't nod at me or my father. He asked who would begin and a man behind me stood up.

"I'm John," he said. "And I'm an alcoholic."

Everyone in the room turned to face him.

They all said, "Hi, John."

My father and I hadn't turned around. It seemed like everyone in the room was looking at us. My father stared at his hands and rubbed his knuckles. I did the same. The man talked about how his job was hard. How he wanted to drink every night when he came home, but he didn't.

He talked about how he used to go out in the employee parking lot at lunch and drink in his car. He said he had been sober for two hundred and forty-seven days. Some of the men clapped.

My father stood up. I thought he was leaving so I stood up with him. He said, "My name is Thomas, and I'm an alcoholic."

I sat down. Everyone said hello to my father. He spoke about how he had no job. He spoke about having no true friends. He told those men he felt like the world had caught up with him.

I heard every word he said. I could have recited them on command. When he sat back down it felt uncomfortable. It seemed like all the men were looking at me again.

The rest of the meeting I didn't hear anything. I watched one man fall off his chair and climb back on. Nobody laughed at him. I saw men drinking cups of coffee and lighting cigarettes. I saw my father get up and eat a doughnut. But I didn't hear a single word.

The next day at school I felt sick. I tried to vomit. The left side of my head ached, then the right. I felt thirsty, but I could barely get any water down. I felt anxious. It wasn't at all how I'd felt when I drank at the oak tree.

I didn't feel better until the end of the week. I had been sleeping every minute I wasn't in class. On Friday I even fell asleep in class and missed my bus. I got about three blocks walking home before my father drove up next to me in his cab. He stopped and got out onto the sidewalk.

"Get in," he said. "I'm headed to a taxi stand past our neighborhood anyway."

I got in. My father's cab smelled clean. There was a pine tree swinging from the mirror.

"I told your mother you aren't really a drinker," he said.

I nodded my head at him.

"Don't prove me wrong," he said.

He turned the radio on. The oldies station was playing a block of Beatles songs.

"I can never tell which one's singing," I said.

"If it's deeper, it's John," he said. "John was the negative to Paul's positive."

The dispatcher called out on the radio for my father's location. My father told her where he was, and she gave him a fare. He stopped the cab.

"Would you mind, Zain, if I let you out here? I should really take this fare."

I got out and closed the door. I waved at my father and he waved back.

My mother was cleaning the house when I got home. She had a bunch of bottles lined up on the coffee table and the hoses were hanging off the vacuum. The house smelled like vinegar.

I went upstairs and did my homework until dinner was ready. My father came home and ate with us in the dining room. My mother made us strawberry milk and she cut strawberries to hang on the sides of our glasses. We talked about what we should cook for Thanksgiving dinner, or if we should maybe just eat at a hotel buffet in Washington.

After dinner, we washed the dishes and played three-handed pinochle. My father kept taking the kitty. Then we went into the living room and my father gave us index cards so we could all guess who shot J.R. When *Dallas* came on, we climbed on the couch together and watched, cards in hand. None of us had thought to guess it was Sue Ellen's cousin. My father had actually written down "J.R."

17

My father didn't drink all weekend. We spent Saturday painting the rest of my bedroom. On Sunday my mother went to an all-day bingo game above the firehouse. My father made us potatoes and onions, and we watched some football. My father even brought the TV from the living room into the TV room so we could watch both of the early games at once.

On Monday I skipped school again. This time, I didn't drink, or steal, or tell lies. I walked all the way from our house to Key Bridge. I crossed Key and went along the canal and found my way up towards Watergate. When I got to my father's CIA buildings, I stopped and took a rest. I sat across the street and watched the gate. The guard never, ever, turned his back. I looked at the brick wall that wrapped around the compound. It was too tall for me to scale.

At lunchtime the gate got busy. Sometimes there were four or five cars going in at the same time. I waited until a van got in the line. It was a white van with the words "U.S. Government" on its side. I stood next to the van and moved when it moved, staying way off to its side and near its middle so the driver couldn't see me out the passenger window, or with his mirrors.

After we got past the gate, I ducked into the parking area. I waited until a crowd of people were entering my father's building and I got in line with them. While they were showing their badges, I stayed down low, out of sight of the guard. I walked with them and then found my way into a bathroom. I didn't know where my father's boss had his office. For a while I sat in a stall hoping he'd come in to use the bathroom. He never did.

No one was in the hallway, so I headed for the elevators in the middle of the building. There was a board with names and office numbers. I didn't know the man's name, but I knew he was international counter terrorism like my father was. I found all the office numbers but no listing of jobs or who was in charge. I remembered the man wore a small gold cross to our house when he came for dinner, but that didn't narrow the names down any. I tried to remember his hat. I tried to remember his accent. I wondered why no one in our house ever used his name.

Then I heard his voice behind me. He was coming in with a lunch crowd and he was talking in the same voice I'd heard him use the day we hung drywall in my bedroom. I got in the elevator with him and his crowd, and I stood near the back. When he got out on the third floor, I waited until the doors started closing and then I slipped out. He was already alone, walking toward the end of a dark hallway. I caught up and walked into his office right behind him. He said hello to a lady sitting behind a thick desk. She smiled at him as he passed. When she saw me I waved at her and kept in step with my father's boss.

I sat down while he put his hat and coat up on a rack. When he sat down he looked straight at me.

He said, "You've been following me since the elevator."

"I have," I said.

"You're Zain," he said. "I was pretty sure it was you in the elevator, but now that I'm sitting here looking at you, I remember you quite well."

"Yes, sir," I said.

He pushed his chair back and swung his feet up onto his desk.

"I know why you're here," he said.

I didn't say anything.

"You want to know who the man is that your father beat up," he said.

"You know about that?"

He stood up and came around to sit on the front of his desk.

"Of course I know," he said. "You did a good thing, Zain, pulling your father off before things got out of hand."

"He was your man," I said. "He was working for you."

"In a manner of speaking," he said.

He walked over to the window and pulled the curtain aside. He looked just like my father when he did it.

"That's not why I'm here," I said.

"Oh? You don't want to know if the man Tom beat is okay?"

I nodded my head yes.

"He is okay," he said. "But he isn't pleased, and neither am I."

He came over and sat down in the chair next to me.

"People go one of two ways when they leave the CIA," he said. "Your father went one of those two ways."

"He didn't leave," I said.

His phone rang. He went to it and put his hand on the receiver.

Then he said, "Wait in the outer office."

I went out and sat in front of his door. I couldn't hear anything he was saying, but I could hear his voice get different than it had been with me. When he opened the door, I almost fell into his office.

"Get up," he said, "and get on with it."

I sat back down in a chair. He stood over me.

"We want my father's job back," I said.

"Who's we?"

"All of us," I said. "Even my mother."

"You've spoken to her about it?"

"No," I said.

He looked at me until I spoke again.

"We don't talk in my family," I said. "About anything."

"You think Tom wants to come back now?"

"I think so," I said. "Yes. Yes, he does."

He went back behind his desk.

"I like you," he said. "But I cannot help you in this matter."

"You can," I said. "If you decide to."

He laughed a little at that. I wondered if he really thought it was so funny. He took out a pad and wrote for a minute. Then he put his pen down and looked at me.

"Tom has some problems now," he said.

"No," I said. "He's sober. And he beat that man because he thought he was being followed. Which he was."

He nodded his head at me.

"Have your father call me and we'll have a conversation," he said. "Much as I enjoy talking to you."

He put his hand out for me to shake. I took it. It was so big I couldn't see my own inside of it.

It took almost three hours to get home. My legs were tired and I kept replaying it all in my head. My mother would be mad at me for skipping school. And I couldn't tell her why I had done it. I spent the walk home, in fact, not knowing what exactly I had done.

I didn't tell my father. I wondered if it would be better not to. His boss might forget, or maybe he'd call my father after a week or two, closer to Christmas, and maybe they'd just start talking.

When Thanksgiving came, I knew I needed to do it. We barely had much of a meal at all. My father said we couldn't afford to waste money. My mother spent most of the day in her room. She told us she had a headache. We ate on our own like it was any other day.

My father and I watched the end of the Cowboys' game together and split a can of cranberry sauce. When it was over, I turned off the TV.

I said, "I think you have to go back to the CIA. I think you need to go back to the CIA."

He got up and turned the TV back on, but without the sound.

"I can't go back," he said. "Zain, don't you think I know the cab thing isn't working?"

I pulled my chair closer to him. He put his hand up like a stop sign.

I said, "You obviously want to go back. Otherwise you would have taken a real job by now instead of driving that broken-down cab."

"You don't know everything," he said. "I looked for jobs all over the place."

"I don't believe you," I said.

"You don't believe me. You don't believe me? You're a real bastard, Zain."

I wondered why he didn't hit me. I wondered if he thought I'd hit him back.

"Zain, let me tell you something. Okay? I applied to insurance offices, hospitals. I applied for every job that analyzes records of any damn kind."

I couldn't look at him. I couldn't watch him the way his face looked.

He said, "No one would hire me. Most of those assholes said I was overqualified. The other ones just didn't want to hire a man who got fired from the CIA."

"They said that?"

"No, Zain. Of course they didn't say it. You've got a lot to learn. You're a smart kid, but you don't know much, do you?"

"I know enough to know you could get your job back."

"How would you know that?"

I stood up and put the chair between us.

I said, "I saw your boss."

He cocked his head to the side.

"You saw my boss?"

"He wants to meet with you. I told him you're sober. I told him you wanted to come back. I told him it wasn't your fault you beat up their man."

My father stood up fast and came at me. He shoved the chair with his left hand and me with his right. I hit the wall to my mother's bedroom so hard that she came out.

"What's going on out here?"

"Nothing," he said. "Nothing."

My father stared at me.

Then he said, "That was their man."

"It was," I said.

He nodded his head. He looked at my mother and then back at me. Then he took the car keys and left the house.

18

M y father was gone for more than a week. He called and told us he needed to take care of some things. My mother kept me home from school to be with her. We didn't talk about what he might be doing.

I paid for our groceries with the money I had left over from my fast food job. I returned the hammer to Ben Franklin's five and dime the same way I had taken it out. I bought a window panel and a caulking gun and fixed the damage I had done to the garage. After it snowed, I went over and shoveled the sidewalk for Mr. Zero's widow.

During the afternoons I watched MTV. At night I watched *One Day at a Time*, *Charlie's Angels*, *Fantasy Island*, and *Taxi*. My mother kept the house clean, and I kept up with my schoolwork. We left the porch lights on day and night.

My father came back ten days after Thanksgiving. At first he didn't say much about it. Then he called a family meeting in the dining room. We sat down together and my father took our hands and he said a prayer. Then he took his hands away.

He said, "I'm going to tell the two of you some things and I need you to listen, because I don't want to say them again."

He cleared his throat and took a sip of his coffee.

"I had to get away to think about a lot of things. I had to straighten out some issues with the cab company, and with ... I needed to think about what it was I wanted to do with my life. With our lives."

He pushed his chair back away from the table. Then he reached forward to get his coffee mug.

"I met with my boss, and with his boss as well. We spoke for a few days, on and off. I made my decision, and we talked about it, and I'm going back into the agency."

My mother inhaled deeply. I could hear her throat catching.

"The only way I could get back in was to take a trip."

My mother put her hands in the air.

She said, "No, Tom. We can't go overseas for three years. I won't do it. I won't."

"Relax," he said. "I know. I know. I made a deal. It's a good deal. For all of us."

He stood up and went behind his chair. He gripped the top of his chair as he spoke. I could still see the punching scars on his knuckles.

"I'm going, by myself, to Iran."

My mother stood up.

"Jesus," she said.

I said it too.

"Not for long. I won't be there for long. I promise."

"When will you come back?"

"I can't say. Betty, you know I can't say. You're lucky they're allowing me to tell you where I'm going."

"Yes," she said. "Lucky."

My father walked over to her. He kissed her on the top of her head.

"This will be over soon," he said.

My mother looked up at him.

"Does this have to do with Reagan? With Bush?"

"I can't say," he said.

"The man takes office in less than a month, Tom, and you're going to Iran and you'll be home soon, but you can't say if it has to do with Bush?"

My father put his hand on my shoulder.

He said, "Why don't you help me pack?"

"Okay," I said.

My mother went into the kitchen, and my father watched her go before turning to go into their bedroom. I could see my mother standing at the window, looking out. I turned and followed my father.

"Grab all my socks and underwear out of that top drawer," he said.

He unpopped his suitcase and laid it on the bed. I tossed everything I found into it.

I said, "I don't want you to go."

My father didn't say anything. He was rummaging around in his closet. I repeated myself. My father put his King James Bible in the suitcase, then opened the drawer of the nightstand. I watched him place all of his spare bullets into a black zippered pouch.

"I have to go," he said. "This is no life."

I sat down on the bed next to him.

"You didn't want to go back in," I said. "I made you do this."

"You didn't do anything like that," he said.

I grabbed his suitcase and threw it into his closet. My father didn't even look. When he was done storing the bullets from his drawer, he pulled out his Beretta and began to unload it.

"I forced you out of the CIA in the first place," I said. "If you guys didn't have me fucking everything up, you'd have gone to Germany."

"Zain," he said, "you don't know everything, you know? Maybe you should just go and sit with your mother. Keep her company."

"No," I said. "You'd be in Germany now instead of risking your life trying to free those hostages."

My father zipped up his bag of ammo, and then he put his Beretta back in its holster.

"Look, Zain, I'm going to tell you this one time. One time. You are not the reason I didn't go to Germany, and you are not the reason I refused to take a trip in the first place."

He stood up and went to the closet to get his suitcase. I watched him refold his socks into little tubes.

He said, "I can't have you thinking you had anything to do with this."

"Why didn't you want to take a trip then? How am I supposed to believe this isn't my fault?"

He put his socks and underwear and gun and bullets into his suitcase.

"You'll just have to believe it," he said.

"Well I don't," I said. "And I never will."

My father slammed his suitcase closed and then slammed closed his chest of drawers.

"Damn it, Zain. I didn't want to go on a trip because I'm on the lists. Okay? Too many people have my name."

He went back to the closet and stood there.

"Fuck it," he said. "Tell your mother to finish packing my clothes. I'm going out."

He grabbed his jacket and left. He said something to my mother on the way out before he slammed the door behind him.

My father came back the next afternoon.

"I have to go," he said.

My father drove us all to the airport, and I sat up front, between them. My father had a government sign for the dashboard, and we parked right out in front of the terminal. My mother bought flight insurance at the kiosk while my father and I watched a cartoon on the twenty-five-cent black and white TVs.

My father told us he didn't want a show, and he warned my mother not to cry.

"This is just another trip," he said.

Then he got on the plane and left us.

On the way home we heard that John Lennon had been shot outside his apartment building. My mother pulled our car off the road.

She said, "I don't know where this world is going."

We stopped off at a pizza place. My father had slipped me a twenty-dollar bill at the airport. He told me to take my mother out for some pizza and to play the jukebox for her. I played five dollars worth of country songs while we waited for our take-out. When we left the restaurant, our songs were still playing.

At home we ate our pizza. Neither of us said a word. When we were done I got up and went into the living room to turn out the lights. I don't know why, but I pulled back the curtain and peeked into the night. I didn't know if I was looking for the guy who robbed my mother, or for some CIA agent to be watching our house. I was looking for something out there in the darkness, something I couldn't quite imagine, just hours away from my sixteenth birthday.

WINTER

19

Christmas came and went without a single word from my father. My mother bought an artificial tree no bigger than she was and put it in the television room. She said she didn't want anyone to drive by and see pretty lights on a tree. She didn't want people standing outside in our yard singing Christmas carols and handing out red and white candy canes.

Without my father, there was no Christmas. We didn't put the wooden airplane his father had given him on top of our tree. We didn't go to the Woolworth's over by the train tracks to look at window displays. We didn't go down to see the National Tree or to shop along the avenues under the lights strung from power lines.

But I knew his absence wasn't the reason. Even when he was home, most Christmas seasons it seemed, we hardly ever did much anyway. But one thing my father had done when he did celebrate Christmas was set up his old Lionel steam train on a three-rail steel track. He had a coal-black engine that smoked and whistled. He had a trolley car that went faster than the curves of the track could handle. He had tiny Plasticville USA people and a plastic railroad station and village houses made of cardboard that lit up from inside. I missed seeing that tiny world under a seven-foot pine tree, and my mother knew it.

My mother bought me clothes for Christmas. She gave me a new uniform for school complete with a blue polyester sweater-vest. She gave me eight pairs of underwear and a half-dozen dress socks. She gave me a new pair of black lace-ups and a shoe shine kit. I gave her a woven leather bracelet I had made at school. She wore it that night, when we went out to

Denny's, but not the week after that.

My father's boss came by early on New Year's Eve. My mother let him in and we sat with him in the living room. A few minutes went by before he said what we wanted to hear.

"Tom will call you tonight," he said.

My mother's teacup stopped rattling on its saucer.

"That's the plan," he said.

"Good," I said. "What time?"

He shifted in his chair and checked his watch.

"Anytime," he said. "I suspect he'll call you anytime now, seeing as it is already New Year's where he is."

"We'll keep off the phone," I said.

"A good plan," he said.

Then he got up, kissed my mother awkwardly on the cheek, and left. He still had his teacup in his hand.

My mother went into her bedroom to wait for my father's call. I went into the TV room and turned on the set. I looked around for New Year's countdowns but it was still too early. I flipped on the news and watched someone interview Dick Clark. Then they started talking about Reagan. There was a man reporting from the Middle East. The transmission was fuzzy. He was talking about the hostages, and how it had been so long now that something was likely to happen very soon.

The phone rang a half ring. Then there was a clatter of plastic and I heard my mother's voice shouting "Hello?" I picked up the other line. My mother was yelling into the phone, but no one was there. She kept repeating herself over and over.

"No one's there," I said.

I hung up my end, then picked it back up to check for a dial tone.

Then it rang. The receiver was already in my hand.

I said, "Hello."

"Zain," he said. "How are you? Where's your mother?"

"She's here," I said. "I'll get her."

My mother was on the line by the time I opened her door. I stood there and watched her back rise and fall as she spoke. She laughed once, but mostly she talked low. Even more than that, she listened.

When she hung up the phone, I wondered if he was still on the line, and I went back to the TV room and picked up the extension.

"Hello," I said.

My father was already gone.

My mother didn't talk to me about what they had said. She told me he was safe, but that he didn't know when he'd be coming home.

I went outside and looked up into the night sky. I wondered if there was one, single star I could see that my father could see just as clearly. I wondered if I'd be studying more astronomy if I weren't going to Catholic school. I wondered if my father hated that he missed both Christmas and New Year's with us. Then I went back to the TV room and I watched MTV's video countdown and Dick Clark and the Times Square ball, and then I went to bed without making a noise.

I watched college football alone on New Year's Day, and my mother went to an all-day bingo game. She brought home Marino's pizza, four big squares each, and we ate until we were sick to our stomachs.

20

Like that, the holidays were over, and I was back at school learning about Christ, and trigonometry, and girls.

We weren't allowed to fraternize at school, even though just about everything we did was co-ed. My father had shown me his yearbook photos of our high school. When he went, the entrances were separated. "Ladies" went in on one side, and "Gents" went in on the other. Most everything was separated when he went. Now they let us learn together, but that was it. If you talked to a girl in the parking lot after school, some nun would come by and just stand there, looking at you.

And most of the parents wouldn't let their daughters talk on the phone to any boys. There were tales of how the girls were subjected to things like album checks. The girl would sit with her mother and father and they would play any new album or 45 she got. They would listen not just to the lyrics but to the rhythms of the music. Anything sexual had to go. The offensive records were snapped in half. Some parents still liked the drama of the bonfire.

My father was different. He told me to listen to anything he owned, except his Confederate records. He had a few 45s he said weren't for listening. He played me once, a novelty record that was ridiculously racist. It was actually printed like a Confederate flag. When I asked him why he had them, he said they were collectors' items, like Confederate money. My mother, he said, had dinnerware from occupied China. And those Norman Rockwell plates.

It was January, as cold as it would get. My mother began playing more and more bingo and started selling Avon products for something to do. I went to school, did my homework, and watched the TV news. I watched when my mother wasn't around to see it. I even read the front section of *The Washington Post*. The last day of Carter's era and Reagan's inauguration were only a couple weeks away. Not much else seemed to matter. OPEC was raising oil prices, and some people were killed in an earthquake in Europe, but I didn't pay much attention. All I wanted to know was what was happening in Iran. I started watching cable news day and night.

Occasionally, they would show footage of the streets in Iran. They showed footage of people in a marketplace. Footage of soldiers. Random shots of the man-on-the-street. Always, I looked for my father.

At school people were beginning to talk. Kids whose fathers were high officials in the military started rumors that the U.S. was about to invade Iran. FBI kids said their fathers knew of terrorists from Iran who were working their way up in American businesses. One kid whose father was a Secret Service man said that Reagan had an eight-man detail protecting him twenty-four hours a day. Another said Reagan had a seriously violent plan in place to free the hostages. I wondered what my father knew. I wondered if I would be spreading my own rumors if he were home.

My mother never even brought up my father except when I went to get the mail. She'd ask if there was anything from him, and I would tell her no.

Then it came. A letter from my father. It was in an envelope mailed from Langley, and the handwriting wasn't his. But the envelope had his name up in the left-hand corner. My mother's eyes opened wide.

"Give that to me," she said.

I gave her the envelope and she opened it fast, slicing her thumb with the edge of the paper as she did it.

"It is a letter from your father," she said.

She stuck her thumb in her mouth and sucked off the blood. I watched her eyes moving up and down as she read the letter.

Then she handed it to me. Most of the page was covered with black ink, with little jumbles of words in between. My mother was saying "son of a bitch" over and over, and "those bastards." All that was left of my father's letter was a line or two about missing my mother's cooking and a reminder to me to keep my chin up at school. But the signature was my father's, and underneath was a final line that said, "Peace Always."

My father's boss called the next day. He talked to my mother for over an hour. When she got off the phone she sat me down at the dining room table.

"The man who robbed me," she said, "was apprehended. Again."

"That's great," I said.

She looked at me like my father did.

"No," she said, "not really. That puts it on me to go to court and testify against him."

I got up and looked outside. I went around to all the windows and then I came back to the table.

"No one's watching us," I said.

My mother shook her head.

"That's why he called you?"

"That's why," she said. "There's no need for them to watch you or me anymore."

"So, then," I said, "why did you talk for an hour?"

"Was it? I hadn't noticed." She got up and poured a cup of coffee.

"You were arguing with him," I said.

"How do you know?"

"Because you weren't raising your voice," I said.

"That doesn't make sense, Zain. But yes, I was arguing with him."

She took a sip of the coffee.

"Cold," she said.

I took her cup and put it in the microwave.

"Don't bother," she said. "Listen. Your father and he spoke about it and he thinks I should just drop the case. Keep our family name out of the papers."

"But that's what you want," I said. "Isn't it?"

"It was. It was. Now I don't know."

"The man he beat up wasn't the robber," I said.

She stood up and put her hands on her head.

"Yes, but your father thought it was," she said.

Then she said, "If I testify, that robber will go to jail much, much longer. We'll have longer to be safe."

"And then he'll be madder when he gets out," I said.

"Either way," she said.

"Either way," I said.

That was the last we spoke of it.

My father's boss called every few days to let us know my father was okay. I wondered if that was something he was allowed to do.

21

A few days before Reagan's inauguration all the rumors in my school had merged into one. Reagan did have a plan to free the hostages. The rumor was that as soon as Carter left office Reagan would come in, Wild-West style, and he would bring the Apocalypse to Iran. Even the kids spreading the rumors were nervous about it. We had all read enough of the Old Testament and studied enough world history to know where we were heading. It got so bad that our Mother Superior called a school assembly to warn us about spreading false prophecies.

I even heard a rumor that Bratton and his crowd were going to skip school to see Reagan's inaugural walk to office. I wondered if Bratton would do something stupid like throw eggs at the limo. I wondered if I should go with him.

My mother and I started to watch the news together. The newscasters outside the U.S. were picking up on the story. The rumors weren't confined to my school. A British newsman said that the Iranian government feared retaliation for the taking of the hostages. He said that the Iranian government saw Reagan as a "cowboy" who was capable of anything. One person they interviewed even referred, on national TV, to the "End of Days."

And so I unplugged all the televisions, and my mother stopped home delivery of *The Washington Post*, and we sat around playing cards. We played five-card stud, and war, and hi-low. We used the pennies my father kept in an old water cooler jug. We played hands where jokers were wild and we tried to figure out a way to play pinochle with only two players.

But mostly we waited. My mother kept me home from school. We took turns cooking, and we cleaned the house like it was springtime.

My father's boss stopped calling. When we tried his office, we got a machine. My mother asked me for my Bible and I gave it to her. She didn't open it. She put her hand on it and she sat on the porch in the cold, and she waited. By the day of the inauguration, we had stopped talking to each other.

We didn't use the sound when we watched the TV news. My mother was afraid we wouldn't be able to hear the phone. So we watched Reagan's big, black limousine push its way through the streets of D.C., and we sat there in silence. The reporters didn't look very happy. The crowd looked very serious. When Reagan showed himself, his enormous smile looked out of place.

My mother picked up a set of needles and started sewing something in blue. I flipped around all the channels. It seemed like they were all using the same three cameras.

The doorbell rang. My mother picked up the phone and looked at me. Then she set it back down. Neither of us got up. The doorbell rang again.

"That lady across the street," I said.

I got up and walked through the length of the house. My mother said something behind me, but I couldn't make it out. I looked through the peephole. I saw the back of a man, then he turned to face me. He had on some kind of uniform. I opened the door.

"Young man," he said, "I have a telegram for you."

I asked him what he meant.

He handed me a piece of paper and turned and walked away.

On the paper was typed the line "I always loved you."

I walked back through the house and looked at my mother. She was knitting fast. I put the paper in my pocket.

"Jehovah's Witness," I said.

My mother nodded her head. I noticed the television was turned off.

"I have homework," I said. Then I went upstairs and stretched out across my bed.

My mother came upstairs to get me. She said we needed to get out of the house. I wondered if I should give her the note. I wondered if it meant anything more than it said.

We drove out of our neighborhood and headed down to where the restaurants were. A lot of people were driving around honking their horns. Some men were standing outside a barber shop waving small American flags.

"Something's happened," she said.

We drove back to the house and ran inside. I pulled the paper out of my pocket to hand to her. The phone rang.

My mother just stared at it. I grabbed it and held it to her ear. My father's boss was already talking. My mother grabbed the receiver and she said, "Yes, yes," and then she put it down on the cradle.

"The hostages are free," she said.

22

That should have been it. My mother told me that should have been the phone call that ended our crisis. She told me that and then she barely spoke to me.

My father did not come home. He had decided to stay overseas. Over the next few years we received postcards that all came from a central output center in London. Eventually the postcards just stopped coming. My father was dead or my father was alive. It didn't seem to matter to anyone. Those few years and the years since seemed to come and go as if they weren't really connected to my life.

My mother remarried a man who did odd jobs in the neighborhood. I left home at eighteen and joined the military for a few years during the end of the Cold War. Wherever I was stationed I looked for my father. In the end, I knew I would never find him.

In the end, I knew I had always been alone.

About the Author

Richard Lee Zuras was born and raised in the suburbs of Washington, D.C., where his father worked as a CIA analyst. Richard earned a degree in writing at George Mason University, then studied at the graduate level at the University of Colorado before earning his M.F.A. from McNeese State University. After doing Ph.D. work at the University of North Dakota, he accepted a teaching position at the University of Maine at Presque Isle, where he is now Professor of Creative Writing/Film Studies Advisor. He has held the Bernard O'Keefe Fiction Scholarship at Bread Loaf, a Wesleyan Fiction Scholarship, and has garnered a Yemassee Prize. His work has appeared in over twenty literary journals, including *Story Quarterly, South Dakota Review, The Laurel Review* and *Passages North*. In his free time Richard enjoys playing sports, watching Oscar-bait films, and spending quality time with his family. He is currently at work on a new novel.

www.ingramcontent.com/pod-product-compliance
Lightning Source LLC
Chambersburg PA
CBHW031607260626
47154CB00020B/1697